Killing was to be good at it.

Kelly Wood had done plenty of both for her government. For the last fifteen years she'd been able to bury her past on a remote Oklahoma ranch in a perfectly normal life—until thirty minutes ago. Now she faced the worst time in her life as she packed only the most necessary items in a black bag. The color reminded her of death, and death was what she used to do best.

With one phone call, her world shattered. She could still hear Janko's voice, deep and smooth as still water, and twice as deadly.

"Hello, KC." She'd almost dropped the phone as her hand trembled. Dread wrapped around her like a shroud. "Hang up now!" had been her first thought. The second had been to run with her kids as fast and as far as possible. It was already too late; she just hadn't known it yet.

From The Shadows

by

Margaret E. Reid

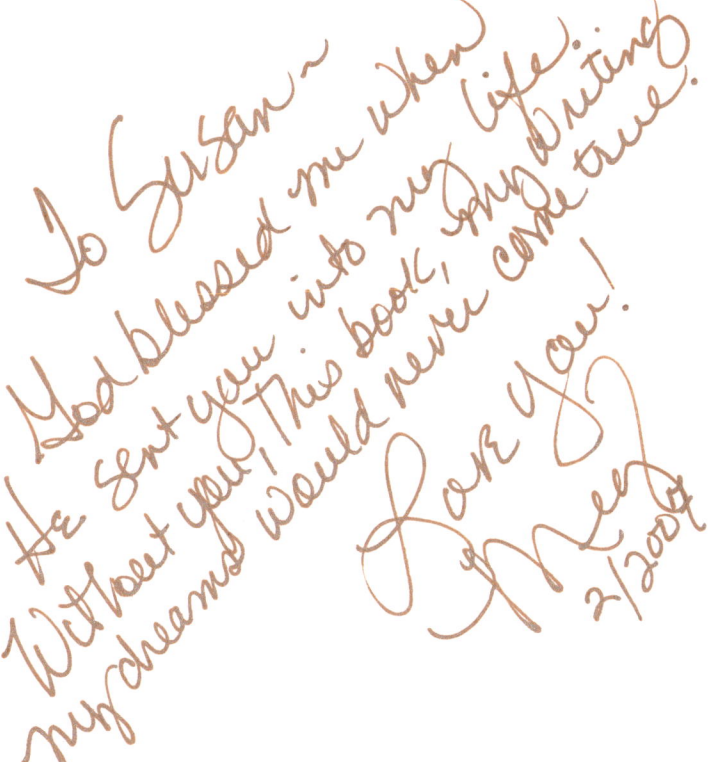

This is a work of fiction. Names, characters, places, and incidents are either the product of the author's imagination or are used fictitiously, and any resemblance to actual persons living or dead, business establishments, events, or locales, is entirely coincidental.

From The Shadows

COPYRIGHT © 2006 by Margaret E. Reid

All rights reserved. No part of this book may be used or reproduced in any manner whatsoever without written permission of the author or The Wild Rose Press except in the case of brief quotations embodied in critical articles or reviews.
Contact Information: info@thewildrosepress.com

Cover Art by Tamra Westberry

The Wild Rose Press
PO Box 706
Adams Basin, NY 14410-0706
Visit us at www.thewildrosepress.com

Publishing History
First Crimson Rose Edition, November 2006
PRINT ISBN 1-60154-025-6

Published in the United States of America

Dedication

To my wonderful family for believing this day would come.

To my daughter, Amy, who never let me give in or give up.

To my son, Tim, who kept me going.

To my sisters of the heart, Marilyn Pappano and Susan Shay, who got me through the tough times, helped me find the magic, then made sure this book was finished.

To Don, my own hero, who inspired, encouraged and supported my dream.

I love you all.

Prologue

The man tore open the padded envelope and a black VHS cassette slide into his palm. Cool and sleek. Glossy and textured. Virtually weightless, yet he trembled under the strain of anticipation. He closed his eyes. He knew he was holding the key that would unlock heaven or hell. As the cassette warmed in his hand, so too, would she become heated by his touch.

Placing the tape under his nose, he inhaled, but it was her perfume he smelled, not the odor of new plastic and expensive cigars filling his office. He nuzzled the tape as if it were her lips he was exploring, then with the tip of his tongue flicked the surface. Bitterness bit back, reminding him of what had gone wrong.

"Dinner!" a female voice screeched. "Did you hear me?"

The doorknob to his study rattled, followed quickly by a fist pounding against the wood. He tightened his hand around the cassette. The cracks sounded like muffled gunshots and the tiny snaps tingled his fingers. His eyes opened, then narrowed as he gazed toward the locked door.

The bitch. Soon it would be her neck beneath his hands. He would enjoy every minute of terror in her bulging eyes, the mottling of her fat cheeks, and the blue tint of her cruel mouth as he squeezed the life from her.

The thought and careful planning of each kill excited him, made him hard, but the actual execution of his mark was when he got his rocks off. Sweeter and more satisfying than sex with a thousand dollar whore. The corners of his recently collagen injected lips twisted into a small smile as he walked to his wall of media equipment.

Yeah, life was great when you got paid for doing the thing you loved. Hell, he had the government's blessing on most of them, but the real money he made was from the other side.

A bank of television screens formed a tic-tac-toe grid. Beneath them, the shelves held satellite receivers, VCRs and DVD players. He had the latest and the best money could buy. Jamming the tape into the closest player, he snatched up a remote and pushed the right buttons as he returned to his desk.

The tape rolled past the credits on a blue screen before fading to black, then a grainy picture appeared. The scene was pandemonium with adults and children running helter-skelter from a growing wall of white. He could hear the panicked "Oh, God, No!" then the heavy breathing of the camera holder until the professionally distant voice over of the news announcer blared.

"The Cherokee County Fair was marred today by the explosion of a steam tractor. A group of school children were watching the demonstration..."

He muted the sound and concentrated on the crowd. There! In the background coming out of the steam was a lone figure. He rewound the tape and played it again. Could that be her? His heart began to thump. His chest tightened.

Leaning across his desk, he rewound the tape a second time to watch. He saw a woman carrying an injured child, but he didn't see the blood and gore. The rasp he heard was his own harsh breathing. He wanted it so badly to be her. The tape jumped up and down as the person behind the camera ran. The woman moved out of the picture.

"Damn!" He hadn't gotten a good look at her, but there was something about that tall woman. As she dashed back into the frame, the camera focused on her. He watched as her lips moved, her gaze searching. A teenage girl lunged into her arms and she encircled her, holding her close. The videographer caught the tender reunion before cutting away.

His heart slammed into his chest with the force of a jackhammer. There was no doubt that was her. In a mere ten seconds, he'd finally found what he'd been obsessing about for the last fifteen years.

He rewound the tape again, then slowed it to frame by frame. There she was—the woman of his dreams. Searching for the best picture, he paused on the last one of her. He drank in her image, but it only made him thirstier for her.

Moving to the front of his desk, he rested against it as he examined the still picture of her and the girl. Before him was the only woman he'd ever really loved. With the click of the remote, he filled each of the nine TV screens with a different picture, zooming in on her face until it was a blur of pixels.

She looked older, her hair was a shade darker, her clothes worn, and she'd put on too many pounds to suit him, but he would change all of that. And anything else less than perfect about her. Nothing but the best for him, and that meant having her.

Bending forward, he opened a cabinet door, then hit the print button and waited for the machine to spit out the picture from the screen. The hum of the mechanism matched the purring in his brain.

As he retrieved the picture, he studied the expression on *his* woman's face as she looked at the girl, and he saw love—a mother's love. They looked so alike, yet so different. But it was the girl's hair, her nose, the shape of her ear that held his attention.

Realization slapped him so hard he almost toppled over.

He was gazing into the face of his own child.

Crumpling the picture, a surge of anger welled deep inside him. Why didn't she tell him? Why didn't she come to him? She knew where to find him. It didn't matter to him if he was already married. Soon that little inconvenience would be resolved.

Contrite, he tried to smooth out the wrinkled faces. Maybe she'd been afraid of the agency. Maybe she'd believed he wouldn't want the child they'd conceived in love. Maybe she'd tried and that bitch hadn't told him.

He stood, straightened his tie, then adjusted the cuffs on his shirt.

It was time to claim what was rightfully his.

It was time to put his family together.

And this time, no one or nothing would stop him from achieving his dream.

Chapter One

Killing was a lot like sex. You didn't have to enjoy it to be good at it.

Kelly Wood had done plenty of both for her government. For the last fifteen years she'd been able to bury her past on a remote Oklahoma ranch in a perfectly normal life—until thirty minutes ago. Now she faced the worst time in her life as she packed only the most necessary items in a black bag. The color reminded her of death, and death was what she once did best.

With one phone call, her world shattered. She could still hear Janko's voice, deep and smooth as still water, and twice as deadly.

"Hello, KC." Her hand trembled and she'd almost dropped the phone. Dread wrapped around her like a shroud. *Hang up now!* had been her first thought. The second had been to run with her kids as fast and as far as possible. It was already too late; she just hadn't known it yet.

"What's the matter? Out of sight, out of mind? I guess you've forgotten me." As he chuckled at his joke, her throat closed.

How could she forget the man who'd shown her how it felt to kill, how it felt to live, the man who'd taught her everything she knew about hatred—and love?

Forget Steven Janko? Hell, no! *Never.*

"Go away, Janko! Stay out of my life." She'd slammed the phone into the base unit only to have it ring again immediately. Did she really think she'd get rid of him so easily? With her heart pounding, she channeled her rage, and her fear, then picked up.

"I have your kids."

In an instant everything stopped. Her breathing. Her pulse. Her life. "You bastard! What have you done?" If he'd been standing in front of her, she'd have killed him with her bare hands.

"What I had to. I need you to eliminate a mark—"

"And if I refuse?"

"You won't. Not if you want your kids back."

"I'll do it, just don't hurt my children." She hated the desperation that had seeped into her voice. Reining in her emotions, she concentrated on his brief instructions, then hung up without another word.

As if it was the last time—and maybe it was—she walked into the living room, stopping long enough to touch the rodeo and sports trophies Ashley and Tyler had won. Those things she'd thought so important yesterday meant nothing without loved ones to share them with.

She turned off the table lamp, leaving the room gilded by the fading spring sunset. The warm glow didn't penetrate the coldness building inside her. She stared for a moment, gathering memories, then went out the door, closing it behind her. The hollow thud echoed in the garage. She wasn't leaving her home, only an empty shell. Her life here, as she knew it, was ending and another would begin, as soon as her children were safely encircled within her arms.

And as soon as she'd killed Janko.

****

Steven Janko sat in the darkest corner of the Talco airport lounge, his attention riveted on the leggy blonde entering the concourse. Kelly, always KC to him, hadn't lost that fluid, purposeful walk he'd found so exciting. And still did.

He pulled hard on the cigarette, glad that his favorite vice hadn't been banned here yet. Waiting for her to arrive had given him too much time to think about her.

About what might have been.

And now, what might be.

"Name's Flo. What can I getcha?" The waitress smacked her gum in time with her pencil tapping on the order pad.

"Stoli, neat."

"Say what, mister?" Her mouth gaped open, exposing the wad of gum oozing between missing molars.

"Vodka, no ice."

She stood for a moment as if to say something, but he'd already dismissed her, barely noticing when she left. He refocused on KC threading her way past deplaning passengers that clogged the narrowed walkway. At almost six feet tall, she was easy to keep track of, but he would have been able to spot her in any crowd. She'd been hot when he'd first met her in college, but time had transformed the debutante into an elegant, beautiful woman.

"Here ya go. That'll be six fifty." Flo placed the drink in front of him and waited.

"I'll run a tab." His answer came out more brusquely than intended.

"Not without a credit card—not at my table, bub."

He took out his wallet, looking through several credit cards before he found the name he wanted to use tonight, threw it on her tray, then took a sip of his drink as she walked away. Stubbing out his cigarette, he lit another one. The swirling smoke reminded him of the years he'd spent playing shadow games with KC. He'd hide in plain sight, watching, waiting for her to catch him, and when she almost had him, he'd vanish once more. He couldn't believe how lax she'd become. As a former agent, she should have maintained a higher standard of security. Why anyone could breach—

"Wanta 'nother?"

"Sure. Keep 'em coming and I'll tell you when to stop."

A smirk touched the corners of his mouth as he

recalled how easy it'd been to enter that rural school and, right under the nose of the harried office secretary, take KC's kids. Watching the two of them walk toward him, he'd noticed they were tall like their mother. But the girl, much like his sister, showed a self-assurance usually not found in someone so young. When she stopped, she kept several feet between them, her blue eyes narrowing with suspicion. The boy stepped right up. He reminded Janko of a puppy, with soft brown eyes, friendly, and gullible.

"Your mother asked me to pick you up," Janko said.

"Cool. Let's—"

"Wait a minute, Tyler." She pulled her brother close, then squared her shoulders. "Why didn't she tell us?"

"I just ran into her and she asked if I minded, but—"

"I don't believe you. What's the password?" she demanded.

What would KC use? He sifted through his memories.

"Oh, come on! If our mother *really* sent you, you'd know."

"You're absolutely right." He stalled a few more moments, watching as her lips compressed into a thin line. Seconds crawled like minutes as he wracked his brain. Hell, what would KC use? As if a light turned on, his mind clicked. "Four-fifty-eight."

She gasped, and he sighed mentally. *Thank you, KC, for using our special code.*

The girl had crossed her arms, then drilled him with an icy glare. "Anybody could have guessed that. What does it mean?"

"I love you. She took the letters I, L, U, and matched them to the corresponding numbers on a telephone." He turned, gesturing to the door. The girl shot him a defiant look when she passed.

As they left the building, Tyler nudged his sister. "Chill, Ashley. We're outta here."

That had been Janko's sentiment exactly as the three of them had gotten into his car.

He twirled his glass until the vodka almost sloshed

over the rim, then set the drink down. KC, the steely emotionless assassin he trained, had become a loving mother. When he'd learned she'd gotten married, then had kids, it damn near killed him. One thing was definite, Janko thought with a deep drag of his cigarette, he certainly wasn't father material. Thank God, he'd never sired any.

"Hey, I get off work in an hour."

He glanced up at Flo. Her eyes gleamed with a hopeful message that he recognized and knew to stay the hell away from. "Sorry, my flight is boarding soon. Could I have my check?"

"Sure."

If she was disappointed, he never knew. His interest centered on KC at the ticket counter, memorizing every detail. Jeans and boots instead of Versace? Not exactly what he expected, but it fit. Her blond hair, down and loose, shaggily framed her face, looking as if she'd just climbed out of the sack after a good long screw. Remembering all the times that they'd made love sent a surge of heat rushing through his body. He could almost feel her silky hair as it had curtained their faces when she lay on top of him. Damn his traitorous body. She still had a hold on him, and it scared him more than any mission ever had.

KC boarded the plane, and he breathed a sigh of relief that she was safe—for now. It seemed he'd spent much of his life worrying about her safety, when truth was, the biggest threat to her was *him*. He'd recruited her, seduced her, and when she'd needed him most—when Osprey failed—he'd sent her away because he'd let the relationship go too far.

It wouldn't happen again.

He signed the credit card slip and took his copy, tossing five dollars on the table as he stood. His cigarette landed haphazardly in the ashtray as his gaze followed her airplane into the sky. Running his fingers through his hair, he stretched the muscles in his back, hoping some of the tenseness would ease. It had only been twelve hours since he'd discovered that she and her children were in danger. A pang of regret nicked at him for snatching her kids, then using them to force her to leave. In route, he'd tried to call, to warn her of the danger, but he never got an answer. She probably wouldn't have believed him anyway. Going to this extreme had been the only way to protect them all.

Even so, would she forgive what he'd done?

Or would she kill him?

****

The lights of the runway grew smaller, then winked out as the airplane soared into the sky. Leaving tonight would have been one of the hardest things Kelly had ever done if she wasn't so worried about her children. She twisted her ring over her knuckle then back until her finger was red. Finally, she clasped her hands together and placed them in her lap.

Where had Janko hidden them? And with whom? Certainly, she knew, they weren't with him. His tolerance for anyone under the age of eighteen was zero. Oh, he'd reassured her several times they were safe, but still they must be so scared. She was. They *had* to know that she'd be coming after them, and would never quit until she found them.

As the plane bucked from turbulence, she idly rubbed the left side of her abdomen, touching the small round scar—a souvenir from Osprey. The physical wound from her last encounter with Janko had healed, but he'd sliced into her soul and scarred her very essence.

Twice before he'd irrevocably changed her life, but now, when he'd taken what she'd held dearest in the world, he'd have to pay. She had to get tough, mentally and physically, and focus totally on the one last mission before her. After that, she would eliminate Janko.

Looking out the window, she saw stars glittering in a cloudless night sky. Stars so close they looked touchable, and she remembered one of the last times she'd been with him. The sky had been dark and starry then, too. Waiting and watching. The same nervous energy consumed her now as it had then...

The shadows of the target house had performed a macabre dance on the waving weeds. Blooming sage scented the cold predawn New Mexico air. Intelligence had forecast warm, cloudy and still. What else had they gotten wrong, she wondered?

Janko's laugh, like a rusty hinge on a loose gate, floated over her earpiece, setting her teeth on edge. "KC, I'll be the point and you be the post, then we'll bag this bad guy. Just like your basketball days at UT."

She cringed. She hated Janko's perpetual happiness, especially at four a.m., in the middle of a field, where she was freezing her ass off waiting for a go. Radio communications were monitored, so she couldn't tell him where to stick Mr. Sunshine, but she'd find a way to get him back. She always did.

Minutes separated plan from execution.

"Ready?"

She sensed rather than saw him look at her. "Yeah."

"I got you, babe."

His go signal grated on her frayed nerves. That was the reason he did it, of course. She couldn't stand that song, but he loved classic rock from the 60's and 70's. Reliving the past, she'd teased as she'd switch radio stations in the car.

"Crimson and Clover."

"I get it. Over and over." His faint screech reached her on the wind. He'd moved.

Clouds drifted across the half moon, shrouding the area in darkness. She waved her team forward as agents from hidden positions converged on the dark house. The camouflage and painted faces made them virtually invisible. KC crept cat-like through the tall grass, her senses sharpening as she closed in. She flipped the safety off her short-barreled MP-5 and pressed her left elbow against the knife in her belt, hoping she wouldn't have to use it this time.

TZZZZZZ BOOM. She'd just taken another step forward when the explosion shattered the night, taking out the men in front of her as gunshots from nowhere and everywhere blanketed the area. She reacted instinctively, flattening on the ground, and watched in horror as bodies, and parts of bodies, rained around her.

With the quick elimination of her target now impossible, she melted into the shadows. Using her riflescope, she assessed the situation. Team one, *her* team, had been taken out by the blast, and to her right, Team two—Janko's team—were all down.

Everything was suddenly quiet...deadly quiet. She tried to get rid of the tinny taste in her mouth and realized that she couldn't. There was no spit. Missions had soured before, but never like this. Oh, God, what had gone wrong? Her men were down. They'd been more than just a team. They were her *friends.* She knew their families, their children.

Shots fired from the house sprayed dirt high into the air. With adrenaline surging through her, she planned her next move. Recognizing Janko's silhouette, even though he wore the same dark clothing she did, she crawled to him. The wind-stirred grass concealed her zigzag track as she covered the twenty or so feet without detection.

"Janko...Janko?" He didn't move. A cry caught in her throat as she saw the blood and dirt that peppered his auburn hair. She tossed her assault rifle to the ground, then checked his neck for a pulse.

"Fumble—Fumble!! Agents down, agents down!" KC screamed into the mike under her vest before the whiz of a nearby bullet forced her back to the ground.

"Where are you guys? Code three, code three!" Why wasn't back up here already? They were still in extreme danger!

In the silence that followed her call came a high-pitched whine that filled her with more terror than the snipers in the house. Ignoring the pain in her side, she threw her body on top of Janko to shield him just as the missile leveled the house. An eternity passed before the debris stopped falling, and before she felt him stir. A measure of relief flowed through her as she exhaled her pent-up breath.

"Hey..." In spite of everything, she smiled, but the smile froze, then disappeared when her gaze locked with his frigid blue one.

"Get off me." His words struck her as brutally as the shove he gave her. She fell back, landing hard on the ground. Anger evaporated her momentary confusion.

"Dammit. What's wrong with you?" His silence infuriated her. Scrambling to her feet, she snatched the black knit cap from her head, releasing her hair.

She glared at him as he slowly stood with his back to her. As he surveyed the carnage and destruction, she saw his shoulders straighten before he turned around.

"You're hurt." Her ire softened, and she reached out to touch the gash on his head. He jerked away, refusing to look at her.

As the sky lightened, she watched the steel curtain that hid his emotions part for a fraction of a second, and that was all she needed to know exactly what he thought. She shook her head with disbelief. "My God, Steven, you think—You think I—No, you're wrong. You have to believe me."

Cars converged on the site, personnel spilling out like ants. Both KC and Janko waved off the medics as they faced each other.

"Only three other people knew about this operation." The hardness in his voice caused her to stiffen.

She squared her shoulders, prepared to battle. "Are you accusing me?" His implication that she'd betrayed him and let her own people get killed pierced her heart. From deep inside her came an eerie keening. She'd trusted this man with her life, with her love. She knew him better than she knew herself—or so she thought.

Apparently, she'd been wrong.

She searched his face for some sign that she'd been mistaken, that he didn't believe her capable of betraying him, for even the slightest hint of trust, but saw only the muscle in his tightly clenched jaw jump as he turned away. It was then that she noticed his white knuckled fists. She felt a lone tear cut through the fine layer of grime on her face, but before she could respond, Arthur Sandusky arrived. She watched as he scrutinized the grisly scene and his mouth tightened, his eyes darkened.

"What the hell happened?"

"We were burned. They knew we were coming. Everything was going good, then it fell apart." She spoke more to herself than to them. "We went strictly by the book on this one. We didn't brief the undercover support and pilots until we were airborne, then we maintained radio silence. No one could have known...so where was the leak?"

"You." Janko's voice dripped venom.

"What proof do you have?" Sandusky's normally calm words were taut with anger and more—frustration. The Assistant Operations Director wasn't usually so open with emotions.

"Operation Osprey took over a year for us to plan. Three of the four people who did that planning can be accounted for. But *she* disappeared last night after our final strategy meeting. Her explanation just didn't add up." Janko never broke eye contact with her. "Where did you go?"

"The same place I told you when you asked last night. It didn't seem to bother you too much then." Like flint on steel, her words struck him, producing sparks from his unwavering gaze. Sandusky's left eyebrow rose slightly.

"Where *did* you go, Kelly?" Sandusky's grim question added another lash to her heart.

"Yes, we all want to know." Janko grabbed her arm, whirling her to stand between the two men. "Why did you go? What did you do? Give me answers, and don't lie. Couldn't you have waited until later? Did you meet or talk to anyone? What was so important that you had to go out, alone at eleven at night, a few hours before leaving on this mission? Tell me, Agent *Garretty*."

She stood silently as his voice rose with each question. The verbal pounding was not the first in her life, but it was the worst. It wounded her spirit.

"Back off, Janko." Sandusky moved him aside. "Kelly, what do you have to say? Can you give us a plausible explanation?"

Her gaze refocused on Sandusky. He looked so out of place in his black Armani suit and handmade Italian leather shoes. But everything had been out of place today, she thought wearily as the ache in her heart spread. "Are you questioning my loyalty, too?" she asked dully. It was so inconceivable that they actually blamed her for Osprey's failure—her lover and her mentor. Her friends.

Digging deep, she found some bit of strength that had survived the last few minutes. "You're going to believe what you want. Nothing I say will change your opinion. So... where does that leave me, Art?"

"Oh, Kelly." Arthur Sandusky looked at his shoes for a moment. "I hate like hell to do this. I wish there was some other way. Lord have mercy, I'm so sorry." He cleared his throat and straightened his tie as if that could somehow soften what he was going to say next. "Agent Garretty, I have no other option than to recommend you be suspended. Pending an investigation, your contract will be reevaluated, then you'll be notified with our findings." He glanced at Janko, who nodded in agreement.

She drew in shallow breaths but didn't flinch. That was it then. She was out, or as good as. She knew the routine. Pegasus always terminated the agents contract, most of the time permanently. And right now, she didn't know if she would be killed. Her life was spinning out of control and there was nothing she could do to stop, or change it.

Regardless of whether she was erased now or later, she *was* a casualty of this failed operation and would never recover.

She looked down, then swayed slightly. On the side of her shirt was a hole no bigger than a pencil eraser framed by a dark streak that disappeared into the waistband of her BDU.

"Are you okay? Your face is a bit gray." From his suit pocket, Sandusky pulled a handkerchief and handed it to her. She mopped her brow. The sun reflected off his balding head, shining in her face as he kept talking. "I know all of this must come as a terrible shock."

A slow seep of blood had soaked into the sandy soil and outlined her boot. She stepped on the telltale stain. Her side burned hotter than the flames of hell. She'd deal with the wound herself, if she got the chance. After all, they'd made it clear she was on her own.

"No, just a few scrapes and bruises," she lied as her eyes bored into Janko. How dare he be her judge and jury? Who had appointed him God? How could he believe that she'd ever compromise an operation? He was the one who'd recruited her, had fallen in love with her, the one person in this world who should have known her best, and now he was blaming her. Her body grew numb, but her heart and soul were shredded. She'd loved him more than life itself, and he'd killed that special part of her. Never again would she let any man get that close to her...

A decrease in altitude snapped Kelly back to the present. She sat rigidly in the seat, fists knotted, sweat beading on her upper lip. The smell of blood still seemed to linger in the air.

As the plane descended, she forced the tension away by focusing on the lights of Dallas growing bigger and brighter while her world grew smaller and darker. The wheels touched down and she centered her thoughts on the job she had to do to get her children back, but Janko was keeping her in the dark. He was the puppet master and she was the damn doll waiting for him to yank her string. *Mother-effin bastard.*

A rush of humid air surged into the plane when the door opened. In the rush and crush to leave, she slouched, blending in with the deplaning passengers just as she used to do so long ago. She scanned the terminal, assessing and dismissing people. Had she really expected him to meet her? Did she really want to see him with his betrayal so fresh in her memory? With her hatred burning white hot?

Of course he wouldn't be here. He couldn't risk his safety, or that of the mission, by personally ensuring someone as untrustworthy as she made it to the next connection. She spotted the agents he must have assigned to meet her. No, he liked a show of force, but geez-louise, did he have to send bubbas? At this time of night, her contacts stuck out in their typical Johnny G-men dark suits, crisp white shirts, and close-cropped haircuts. They stood against the wall, with their arms folded and wearing identical Ray Bans, inspecting each passenger that came off the plane.

Somebody really needs to write a memo and tell'em not to wear sunglasses at night.

She walked past them directly into the restroom. If they weren't able to spot her immediately, she figured she'd let them cool their heels for a little bit longer. She took her own sweet time freshening up.

The agents hadn't moved, and didn't pay her any attention until she asked, "You guys from the Farm?" They didn't answer.

After displaying every picture ID she owned to them, she and her escorts left the terminal by a side door, where a waiting car took them across the tarmac to an unmarked hanger. From deep within the darkness purred a Challenger 60, a cream-over-navy twin turbine jet. As she climbed the stairs between her *feebe* escorts, she shook her head and muttered, "Janko still goes first class."

The interior of the jet looked more like a living room

with plush dark carpet, an overstuffed couch in navy leather under the far set of windows and a matching chair to the right. Cream curtains flanked the many windows. The faint scent of vanilla blended with the rich aroma of fine leather. Past the couch, captain's chairs circled a round table and at the rear of the plane, a swaged drape revealed a bedroom that belonged in *House Beautiful*. The bolts at the base of the furniture and the seatbelts were the only clues that they were on an airplane. At least, this part of the trip would be comfortable.

"Hey, Slick," Kelly said to the taller of the two agents. "Do I get to know where we're going?" She noted the silent exchange of glances between them, then rolled her eyes in disgust.

"Ma'am, could you have a seat? You'll be briefed as soon as we reach altitude." Slick gestured to the armchair before he nodded a salute, then joined his partner, already seated at the table in back.

Dropping her bags at the end of the sofa, she sank into the deep chair, buckled her seatbelt and waited. *Lighten up. Being a bitch will only piss them off.* She wielded flippancy and sarcasm like sword and shield. Too bad she couldn't get in a few pokes at Janko, but there was nothing to do but sit tight until he contacted her. But when? Where?

Her heart grew heavy. She wanted her children back, needed answers now, or she'd go insane and take everyone with her.

She was so absorbed in her own thoughts that the quiet smoothness of the jet's take-off and leveling went unnoticed until Slick handed her a sealed "Eyes Only" folder. Her gaze raked the young man from the top of his perfectly cut dark hair, the slight five o'clock shadow, the starched white shirt, deep burgundy tie and blue-black suit, down to the spit shined polish of his black shoes. He bore the cookie cutter features the FBI wanted. "Where's the tape recorder?"

"Ma'am?"

"You know, the tape recorder that self-destructs. 'Your mission, Mr. Phelps, should you choose to accept.'"

No smile.

"Slick, don't they teach tension breakers where you trained?" Kelly mimicked his stony expression. "You know you're supposed to put me at ease during this flight."

"Yes, ma'am."

"Name's Kelly, not ma'am."

"Yes, ma'am. If you need anything else, give me a call."

Sure I will. She watched him walk stiff-backed to his seat before she ripped open the packet where Janko's name appeared to the left of the Pegasus logo. Her eyes scanned across the page, picking out the words *reactivation, covert mission, elimination* from the hastily handwritten letter. But there was no real information, not much more than what he'd told her over the phone. Why did he need her? Pegasus had younger, slimmer—she cringed inwardly—faster, and more efficient agents than her. There had to be one hell of a reason that Janko would want her back.

She closed the file. Unlike Mr. Phelps on TV, she had no option. Peter Graves had never turned down a mission, and neither had she. Her work had defined her life and she'd loved it, most parts of it. She hadn't wanted to leave Pegasus, especially like that. Now, she didn't want to go back, certainly not to work with Janko. Her priorities had changed.

Children had a way of doing that.

Chapter Two

The screech of wheels on the runway woke Kelly. Sitting up, she unwrapped the blanket covering her, amazed that she'd slept at all, and even more amazed that she'd never noticed the Farm Boys had checked on her during the night. As she stood to fold the blanket, she realized that the stiffness in her back went all the way to a crick in her neck.

God, I am getting old. She sighed and pretended not to notice the cautious approach of her young escort, but she'd heard him unbuckle his lap belt.

"Good morning, Agent Wood," he said stiffly.

"Oh, morning to you, Mister, ah, Bond?" Shaking her head at her own obscure joke, she watched the man's nervous habit of looking away from her. What had he heard about her? That she'd been one of the best operatives that Pegasus had employed? Or that she was one of the oldest?

The small jet rolled to a stop next to a jeep on the deserted tarmac. "We've landed. Are you ready?" the young man asked as she gathered her few things.

What a question. Sure, she was ready, and of course, she wasn't. That was why she was at a secret facility to cram in as much training as she could before getting down to work.

"Good luck." His tone held no more emotion than his face.

Whatever.

She gave him a curt nod and waited for him to swing

open the hatch. A blast of tepid, humid air met her. Reaching into her bag, she pulled out a pair of sunglasses and walked down the metal steps to a squat military jeep. Climbing in the passenger side, she mumbled, "I don't imagine you talk much more than young Mr. Bond, huh?"

The driver's mirrored sunglasses prevented her from reading his expression. "Ma'am, the colonel is waiting for you in his office." The jackrabbit takeoff of the jeep halted any further attempt at conversation.

As they drove, she eyed her driver, a sergeant with his neatly creased khakis that screamed 'lifer', then turned her attention to their surroundings. They'd landed at an old military base that she guessed had probably been decommissioned during the heavy defense cuts in the 80's. Scrawny trees twisted around brush that encroached on the runway, and the buildings that came into view were dilapidated. Hangars, their doors fully open, no longer contained airplanes or helicopters, nor the men that tended them. Tall grass surrounded the rows of Quonset huts whose paint now peeled under a warm spring sun. Blank traffic lights guarded vacant streets. The bright yellow heads of dandelions had pushed through the cracks and dotted the center of the road and empty parking lots.

But appearances could be deceiving. She'd staked her life on that too many times. Just because the lights were off didn't mean no one was around.

The jeep came to a stop, drawing her back to her immediate surroundings. They'd parked in front of a building no more impressive than the rest. There was nothing to hint at who—or what—awaited her inside.

She climbed out and was reaching for her bags when the driver stopped her.

"Leave them. You'll be going straight to those barracks after your briefing here." He pointed to a rusty metal hut to her left, then to the front door, centered on the building at the top of four rickety stairs. "The colonel's office is down the hall and to the right." With his prepared speech finished, he put the jeep in park, then marched away.

Yeah, his friendliness had been overwhelming, she thought as she entered the building. She stood still for a moment as her eyes adjusted from the brilliant sun to bleakness. The building smelled unused and musty. Beige walls, dingy and water-stained, closed in on her sense of desolation. The only sound she could hear was her own heart beating. Were her children in a place like this or worse? Where had Janko put them?

Straightening her shoulders, she started down the dark hallway. Her booted footsteps echoed and drowned out the sound of her heart, but not the pounding. Turning the corner, she saw light seeping around a partially open door. The force of her knock made the door groan in protest as it swung wider. The reception area—barren except for a hulking metal desk—mirrored what she'd seen of the base.

"Is that you, KC?"

The voice niggled at the back of her brain. Only a handful of people had ever called her KC, and none of them had been a colonel. So who was he and how much did he know? The Farm boys had used her married name; the sealed files had shown Garretty.

"In here."

It bothered her that she couldn't place a face with the name as she crossed the reception area to the inner office. The man remained looking out the window as she entered. The camouflage uniform fit tightly on his portly body, and his white hair sprouted in all directions, reminding her of her son's clay creations squeezed from her garlic press. The aroma of a sweet smelling cigar lingered.

"Murph!" She dropped her purse and threw herself at him.

He turned in time to catch her. Although she was a head taller, he picked her up in a bear hug. "Ah, girl, you're a sight for sore eyes. I've missed you."

She hugged him tighter. The people she'd left so long ago had been her family. Her boss, Arthur Sandusky, had been like a brother to her, and Mike Murphy had been more of a father than her own. Murph had coddled and pushed, berated and encouraged, trained her mentally, physically and technically. If he'd been on site when Osprey failed, she'd never have been cashiered.

She held him at arm's length. "Colonel? What gives? We didn't hold rank in Pegasus."

Murphy motioned to a chair. As he took his own seat, his demeanor grew more serious. He picked up a pen and twirled it between his fingers. "KC—"

"I go by Kelly now."

He smiled faintly. "Kelly Carleen. I always did like that fine Irish name. By God, KC—Kelly, you matured into the beautiful woman Betty said you would."

Kelly dipped her head in a silent thank you, then searched his face. "Murph, what are you doing here?"

"Osprey's failure had a ripple effect throughout Pegasus. Positions, personnel, even the way we reported to the government all changed. These days information comes and goes only through one man, Control. As the top of the pyramid, all decisions, from what ops are run, down to how many pencils are bought, go through him. Janko's field experience got him reassigned to head of operations while Art became head of personnel and recruiting. There were no more joint strategy sessions, and after the way I saw how Janko's hand were tied... " He let his voice trail. "Things just weren't the same after you left. The new missions consisted merely of stealing stuff from other agencies or foreign government, and weren't always successful with the new candy-boy agents. Retirement looked good, but I came back to work a few years ago. The Army needed me and I needed them after Betty died."

"I'm sorry, Murph. I didn't know." She reached across the desk and lightly touched the framed photo of a middle-aged couple in Hawaiian print shirts.

"Breast cancer." He paused. "I wanted to tell you, but

they sealed your files. Even I couldn't hack into the system."

"Yeah, well, Janko did. He forced me back in by stealing Ashley and Tyler, my kids." She couldn't stop an involuntary shudder. She blamed herself for allowing her kids to be such an easy target. "He just walked into their school and took them. Didn't try to disguise his appearance, and even left his name, Uncle Steve."

"Janko always did have brass balls." He suppressed a grin. "You'll get them back, Kelly." He paused for a brief moment, then shook his head. "The girl who swore she'd never has one of each? How old are they?"

"Tyler is twelve, tow headed, just like I was. He's strong as an ox, built like a linebacker and a crack shot. Ashley—" her voice caught and she reminded herself to maintain control "— turned fourteen last Saturday." Her mind focused on her kids as she always saw them, happy and easy going. How were they going to be after she got them back?

"Do you know where they are, Murph?" She tried to keep the begging out of her voice.

"No, but if Janko has them, then they're safe."

"Why am I here?"

"I don't know. Janko called to see if I had a training session going on. Told me he had someone who needed updating and physical conditioning ASAP." He spread his hands to indicate their accommodations. "Here you are."

What did Janko have planned for her that he couldn't, or wouldn't, tell Murph? And what did he mean physical conditioning? Years of riding her horses had kept her in shape, or so she thought, and it didn't take that much conditioning to pull a trigger. So what was the big deal? Just another hoop that she had to jump through for Janko? Kelly pushed the rising anger down, promising herself that Janko would pay for this.

"As soon as you get settled in, come back so we can discuss your schedule over breakfast. Ah ah—" He stopped her protest with his raised hand. "Not debatable.

You will eat because I'm planning to work your butt off." With a grin, he eyed her backside. "You'll be back in college playing form in no time."

"Promises, promises." *As if that was possible.*

He walked her to the door. "Damn, it's so good to see you. I never dreamed I'd get to again. Now, hurry. I'm hungry."

She hugged his beefy neck, retrieved her purse, and quickly left the building. Hopping in the jeep, she revved the motor, dropped the shift into drive and shot out of the parking lot toward the barracks Sarge had pointed to.

A wave of warm stale air rushed out when she opened the barracks door. Kelly dropped her bags as the stuffiness of the cavernous room filled with rusting metal cots assailed her. Dust motes, illuminated by sunlight filtered through grimy windows, hung in the thick air. She crisscrossed the room, opening as many of the windows as the passage of time and slapped-on paint would allow. A breeze stirred the trapped sunshine and a wisp of hair fell across her eyes. She pushed it aside, grateful for a bit of coolness. Turning, she noticed the trails of her footprints on the floor.

Don't bother cleaning, I'll be gone in a few days.

At the far end of the room was a door that she assumed to be the latrine. What it might be like filled her with apprehension as she pushed in the door. Surprisingly, it wasn't as bad as it could have been, but she opened the small window to let it air before going back into the main room.

The rows of empty beds and lockers standing sentinel against the walls reminded her of all the years she'd spent at summer camp. An old ache came with the memory that while camp had kept her safely away from her father for a few weeks, she had always worried about her mother. "Camp Misery" had taught her how to escape, to cope, to utilize people. This camp had lessons to teach, too.

On the bunk closest to the door, Kelly found two

white sheets and a blanket. A couple of mattresses sagged in the corner. Examining each, she picked the best one, which wasn't so great, shook it, and coughed as a cloud of dust enveloped her. She walked to the middle of the room where the breeze was the strongest, tried the cots and selected the one that squeaked the least. She made her bed, not a wrinkle or fold out of place, then smoothed the blanket over it. Some things a girl never forgot.

Too bad her clothes weren't in as good shape. What she pulled from her gear bag looked as if could have come from under Ashley's bed. Thinking about her daughter caused the sting behind her eyes to increase. Since the kidnapping, she'd found a new perspective on dirty clothes and messy rooms. She hung up a few garments, then left the rest piled on the bed. With a sigh, she closed the locker and walked back to find Murphy for that breakfast he'd promised.

She found him waiting outside his office building, tapping his foot. Although food was the farthest thing from her mind, it wasn't so with Murph—or ever had been, as evidenced by his bulging belly.

"It took you long enough. Did you get set up?" He came down the rickety stairs and met her at the cracked sidewalk. "The mess hall, such as it is, is just across the street. Sarge isn't going to wait much longer. Don't know why I've put up with that grouch for so many years." As they walked, Murphy shook his head, then added with a lopsided smile, "Guess 'cause he's the only one who can put up with me." His belly shook as he chuckled.

The mess hall fit the rest of the base. Two tables near the double metal doors had six chairs around each, making the room seem larger than it was. The gurgle and burp from the coffee maker echoed against the bare khaki walls. The linoleum floors were scarred and pitted by years of serving military personnel food that was not always as palatable as what was in front of her now. Kelly nibbled at her plate of food while Murph plowed through his. On the end of the table, she noticed the stack of booklets.

"Are those for me?"

In between bites he said, "Yes, your reading material. Specs on the equipment we'll be using throughout this training session. You're already a day behind the other guys. But, I know you'll be up to speed soon enough."

"Just who are these other guys?" Not that she really cared, but she wanted to be prepared if they weren't who they seemed to be. *Suspect everyone, trust no one.* That was her new motto, and a good rule to live by.

"Three FBI and two ATF."

"Exactly what type of training am I going to be getting?" She raised one eyebrow at him quizzically.

"Don't you remember Old Agent School, my girl? Now you'll be going through what you laughed at in your twenties." His grin was mischievous.

Kelly couldn't silence a groan as memories of the way she and Janko had danced circles around the old bubbas they'd been required to retrain washed over her. At twenty-four, she'd never dreamed that she'd get old. Hell, she'd never dreamed of becoming a mother, or that her children would be kidnapped. *Damn you, Janko. This is all your fault for getting me into this. There could have been some other way.*

The little appetite she'd managed to stir up dissolved as she looked at the grease that had congealed around the sausage and watery scrambled eggs. She pushed her plate away, then reached for the stack of booklets.

"Are you through? Food's not that bad." Murphy speared the two remaining sausage patties and a piece of toast from her plate. "Did you ever learn to cook or just marry one?" His laughter filled the empty room as Kelly shot him a scornful look.

"I have two kids who can devour a hundred dollars worth of groceries in a matter of hours. I learned a lot of things living on a ranch, and, yes, cooking was one of them." She'd give anything to be back in her own kitchen, making Ashley and Tyler's favorite meal of chicken fried steak, homemade mashed potatoes with thick cream gravy, fresh green beans and salad. The ache in her chest made it hard to breathe.

"Take the rest of the morning to read. Sarge will bring you some fatigues to train in. Get familiar with the obstacle course this afternoon. Dinner is at six."

Not wanting Murph to know how desperate her situation was, she avoided looking at him and nodded. Her chair scraped the floor as she stood, then walked out the door. She knew she'd not see him again until morning.

****

Kelly awakened suddenly, her body shaking. She had to keep the panic and the heartache locked away and not give in to the sheer terror of her dream. If she didn't, she'd collapse into tears, screaming, pleading, begging anyone for her children's safe return, then she'd be no good to anyone—not herself, and certainly not them. But sometimes, oh, God, sometimes a little bit of the fear slipped out and threatened her control—her sanity.

Only a small sliver of moon peeked through the dirty windows, but she didn't need its light to see the time—3:10 a.m.—glowing on her watch. With sleep not returning, she might as well start toughening up. Rolling from her cot to the floor, she began to do push ups, using the physical exertion to banish the nightmare. Her muscles, unused to the exertion, screamed in protest, but her mind refused to listen. When her trembling arms quit, she turned on her back and started endless repetitions of crunches until sweat soaked her clothes.

Outside, the stars winked out as the eastern horizon started to lighten. She jogged down the sidewalk in front of her barracks, not knowing where she was going, only following one concrete path after another. By the time the trail led her back to the barracks, dawn had broken over the tree line.

Stumbling into the shower, she sagged against the mildewed tile and closed her eyes. Five minutes, ten minutes, half an hour, under the streaming water now turned cold, brought her no relief. The tortured faces of the children from her nightmare continued to haunt her.

Badly in need of coffee and a cigarette, she finished her shower, dressed in baggy camouflage fatigues and used the walk to the mess hall to regain her calm. She poured a cup of coffee and headed down the long corridor, following the echo of loud male voices broadcasting their location.

Kelly paused in the doorway before entering the conference room turned classroom. Tables loaded with equipment lined the perimeter of the room and school desks were set around a chalkboard. Standing as a group, the men stopped their conversation and pivoted to watch her as she walked in.

The small hairs on the back of her neck rose as waves of hostility and resentment reached her. The dirty walls of the pea green room seemed to grow longer and taller, making her feel small—and damn, she hated anything or anybody that made her feel small. Already on edge, she sat at the desk farthest away and lit a cigarette, daring any of them to tell her no.

Through the steam from her coffee, she assessed her fellow trainees, all younger, possibly newly promoted. Were they John Wayne, Dirty Harry or James Bond? She picked out the three FBI agents. Definitely Dirty Harry types. They were fully rigged in their battle dress uniforms of all black T-shirts over combat trousers, with webbed belts that held their pistols in regulation issue holsters on the right and magazines of extra ammunition on the left. The ATF guys were dressed in navy BDU's. In her camouflage, she was definitely out of place. Only the belt that should have held her service revolver in place was the same as the others.

Murphy strolled over to her. "Good morning—or is it? You look like hell. Did you sleep at all?"

No way would she admit to the nightmares that haunted her. "Yeah, I got a little sleep."

"I hope you ate something this morning because

you're not living on coffee and cigarettes in my camp."

"Cute, Murph. You can make me do almost anything but eat at seven a.m. The smell of food this early makes me green."

"Suit yourself." He looked at her like a disappointed parent. She shrugged her shoulders, as her teenaged daughter often did with her, then stared at a water-stained ceiling tile until he moved to the front of the room.

He cleared his throat to begin class. "Today's punks know more than we do about how to circumvent our protective measures. These gangs train day in and day out, while once a month law enforcement gets maybe a few hours weapons practice and no hand-to-hand combat. At the far table is the latest in body armor. This is yours to be used later this week, when we update your hand-to-hand skills. Hand combat has been glossed over for years and I'm sure all of you—" Murph looked directly at her "— can use the refresher as well as weapons practice."

A heat she hadn't experienced in years centered in her belly as memories of hand-to-hand sessions with Janko came rushing back. Those sessions had turned into so much more as they battled to see who would get to be on top. Being toe to toe, or hip to hip, circling, waiting for the precise moment to take the upper hand, had excited her. The rush of adrenaline, whether she'd done the pinning, or been pinned, had been the same. Her skin tingled now as it had when the weight of his body had covered hers. They'd exchanged kisses, hot and lusty, instead of kicks, and their hands had sought vulnerable spots to tenderly caress instead of punch. In an exercise that had ended pleasurably for them both, he'd trained her to find and exploit a man's weakness. *All* of them.

Murphy had resumed his lecture, pointing out more equipment on another table. The material that she'd read yesterday began making sense as he explained the technical side of new computer programs and communication devices. When he instructed them to examine the equipment, she picked up a board camera. It was no larger than one square inch, no thicker than a pencil, and required only a pin dot to watch a whole room. She and Janko used to have so much fun hiding these cameras where they were never detected.

Damn you, Janko! I loved my job, just like I loved you.

As the memories overwhelmed her, the room seemed to close in around her. Her chest tightened, and her palms were sweaty. She couldn't afford to show weakness in front of these people. Without a backward glance, she strode out of the room and down the hall, her footsteps echoing the loneliness in her heart. As soon as she stepped into the bright sunlight, she dug out a pack of cigarettes from the depths of her cargo pocket, and shook out three instead of one. The pressure behind her eyes began to build, making her fingers shake as she fumbled with the lighter.

A hand taking away the lighter made her jump.

"Here, let me. Is there anything wrong?" Murph cupped his hands to protect the small flame.

After lighting it, Kelly shook her head. "Just needed to exorcise some old demons." She smoked her cigarette, as Murph eased down onto the wooden steps. Expertly flicking the butt some ten feet into the street, she reached for another one.

"You know smoking is bad for you." Murph held the flame steady once more as she inhaled deeply.

"Yeah, I plan to quit soon—soon as I get my kids back." She watched the smoke disappear in the breeze that whipped around the dilapidated mess hall-classroom. God, how she missed her children.

"Betty never could get me to stop smoking cigars, even while she was lying there dying."

Kelly reached over and squeezed his hand. It surprised her when Murph didn't let go, so she sat on the step below him, her back pressed against the railing.

"It wasn't fair that she was taken away from me just when we were beginning to enjoy each other again. You know, when you've been married for so many years, the bloom of that first romance fades—with time, with kids. Then after the kids are grown and on their own, some couples split up because they no longer like or even know each other. But Betty and me... While I'd been busy trying to save an ungrateful world, she'd been raising our four kids and improving herself. I found myself having to court her and win her back—and I succeeded. After all we'd been through, we fell back in love. And honestly, I loved her more than when we were first married. Then to lose her like that..."

It had broken his heart. She knew the exact roller coaster ride of emotions. She'd lost Janko just when she'd thought things were going so right for them.

With a sigh, Murphy seemed to set his sorrow aside. "Ah, lass, your children are fine. I know it in my old Irish heart. Trust Janko one more time."

She stared at the weeds that widened the cracks in the sidewalk. If she looked at him, she'd dissolve into tears that she could neither afford to shed nor let show.

"Put out that cancer stick and help this old man up. I'm not as spry as I used to be."

She ground her cigarette under her boot, kicked the butt into a crack, then reached out to Murphy. He got up slowly, unsteadily, and she held on to him until he was ready to walk back to the building. In the ensuing silence she wondered if she would live long enough to need help getting up, and whether there would be anyone to give it.

The men continued their work, not bothering to look at her when she came back in the classroom. She shook off her melancholy and slipped on her professional mask. At another table, she found a small gun made of Polyresin. It could have been one of Tyler's toys, except for the flesh tone color. It handled like a toy too, light and sturdy, virtually disappearing within her hand. The barrel could easily be mistaken for an outstretched finger when she closed her grip. An assassin's dream. Closing her eyes, she palmed the gun—warm, and oh, so right in her hand. The perfect killing weapon that she and Janko could have used when they had worked together.

She'd seen him kill and never twitch a muscle, then later make love to her for hours. Had killing fueled the need to engage in the act of procreation? Or had he just needed to feel another warm body next to his?

Sighting the gun on the blank pea green wall, she didn't see the outline of where a picture had once hung, but Janko's face smiling at her as they made love.

Steven, you threw away what you should have kept.

She dreaded seeing him again, but knew that the hour of their meeting was drawing closer. Pain she could no longer suppress welled up and the click of the trigger reverberated down the long room. The sound of silence reached her as she placed the gun back on the table, then turned to see Murph walking toward her.

He put his hand on her shoulder and leaned in close. "Plastics, my dear, that's where the future is." Turning to the others, "Now that the lass has found Honey, hold her up for everyone to see. Deadly cute both of them, wouldn't you say?" His wink to her was conspiratorial.

"Very similar to the Ruger Mark II, except now the barrel, slide and springs have been made of composite polymer. Virtually undetectable. With a two-inch barrel and five shot magazine that can hold either .22s or specialized plastic bullets, this baby is the perfect traveling companion. There's no trail to follow because this weapon is designed to be burned after firing the magazine. The spring and slide composites break down after ten rounds. Ready to try her out, Kelly?" Murph dismissed the class to the firing range.

A Humvee waited outside to take them to the range. When she climbed in, she recognized the driver as the same man who'd picked her up yesterday. Murphy settled himself in the front seat then introduced the driver as Sergeant Green, who'd be their firearms instructor.

A man of many talents, she thought to herself as they rode to the back region of the base. He seemed to be more than Murphy's chief cook and right hand man. Not that she cared if Sarge had become Janko's replacement. She wanted only to get her training then be gone.

The firing range was not what she'd expected as she exited the vehicle. Most ranges were devoid of vegetation, but vines had snaked their way from the forest perimeter over the earthen berm to the cracked cement walk. Stations had been marked out by removing the strangling vines from six of the twenty rusty target stands. A long table of unpainted pine, still smelling new and fresh, looked out of place behind the firing line.

She walked to the last prepared target on the range, distancing herself from the others. Straightening the boxes of ammunition on the table, she noted the caliber of each, and apprehension flowed through her. It had been such a long time since she'd fired a pistol, or any gun. So long since she'd had a reason. Now Janko had given her one.

Sarge's gravelly voice drew her attention to the instructor. "There will be no firing until I give the command. Your evaluation for each exercise will be pass or fail. There is no more shoot to wound. Out in the field, it's kill or be killed. Simple as that." He marched while he talked, never making eye contact with his trainees.

How often had Janko pounded that same philosophy into her head? And not only with guns, but in the way she handled a knife, garrote, even her hands. He'd taught her how to kill—without noise, without emotion—and he'd taught her well.

Sarge barked orders to begin. She did as instructed, putting on safety glasses with amber lenses, and the range took on a soft golden glow. After pulling on the ear protectors, she adjusted them to fit comfortably around the earpieces of her glasses, and wished she could suppress the ache in her heart as easily as the protectors suppressed the noise from the range.

The polymer gun nestled into the web of her right hand—light and well balanced—like it had been made specifically for her. She flicked her thumb on the magazine release, and it slid noiselessly into her left palm. The plastic bullets looked so innocent, but were deadly at close range.

In one smooth motion, she lined front and rear sights with the target, exhaled and pulled the trigger. Her first shot was a flyer, missing the target low and left of center. Adjusting her aim, she squeezed off another shot. Better, but not good enough.

The last to finish the exercise, she knew by then just what to expect of Honey, and herself. Honey was an appropriate name for something so smooth, sweet and quiet. Too bad she'd probably never get a chance to use it.

"Pass," Sarge barked as he replaced her targets.

She didn't care about her scores. Real life was real life, and what you scored on the range meant nothing. The looks she got from the men told her they didn't agree. To them, she was just a woman, and wasn't expected to be—or even capable of being—as good as a man.

The MP-5 thrust in her face made her straighten her shoulders before she accepted the assault rifle with both hands. She jammed the magazine into the bottom of the rifle until it clicked, slipped the strap under her left arm, and waited for Sarge's command.

"Ready on the right? Ready on the left? Ready center?"

Slight head bobs were the only answers Sarge got.

Kelly chambered the first round, raised the MP-5 and stared at the shaded blue silhouette of a man through the scope. Shooting at a target was nothing like shooting a person. She could still see the face of the first man she'd killed. He'd looked her in the eye, knowing there would only be one person walking away that day, and it wouldn't him. She'd made sure of that.

She brought the weapon up, sighting the cross hairs in the scope with the center mass of the target, then fired the first round. A black speck appeared in the smallest circle. With each shot, she relaxed as the rifle became like an extension of her arm. After her tenth round, the middle of the target was one large ragged hole.

Sarge marked her target, then handed her a longer ammo magazine. She flipped the thirty round magazine in her hand, noticing that oil and residue stained her palm.

"Let's rock and roll."

Firing an assault rifle on full automatic was thrilling, and she blocked out the rest of the class as a surge of excitement raced through her. Conscious thought ceased as fire from the end of the barrel flamed and the spray of bullets chewed up the target. In less than a minute, her magazine was empty.

The air, tainted with smoke and gunpowder, stung her eyes and clogged her nose. She tried to hold back the images of that early morning in New Mexico when she'd emptied four magazines trying to save her men. Her heart was pounding, her breathing rapid and shallow, as she ejected the magazine and groped in an empty pocket to find another. Tears pooled at the bottom of her glasses. Strong hands pulling at her MP-5 brought her nose-to-nose with a craggy weathered face, and back to the present.

"Stand down, Agent Wood," Sarge said quietly.

No angry words followed, but in that brief exchange of looks, each knew the other had experienced firsthand the death and destruction the weapon could cause.

She released the rifle, then walked to a bench where a bright orange water cooler sat, squat and glistening. As she got a drink, her arms ached as badly as her heart. Riding horses had never taxed her strength as much as this forty-five minutes of range practice. But no amount of physical pain would keep her from doing *whatever* it took to get her kids back. Never give up or in, she'd been taught, and she wouldn't.

To get her children back, she would send Janko to hell... and leave him there.

Chapter Three

Janko knew it wasn't the smartest thing in the world for him to go home to Seven Oaks, but the thought of KC's kids, scared and not knowing what was going on, nagged at him. After all, if they were *his* children...

He rubbed the back of his neck. From the moment he'd found out that KC and her children were targets, there'd been no time for sleep. He'd cut it close, getting them out of Oklahoma just in time. The bomb that destroyed her house had come as no surprise to him, and with just a few phone calls, he'd be able to use it to his advantage. Maybe this was the break he'd been waiting on.

When KC found out. As if she didn't hate me enough already... He let out a low whistle. *She'll probably kill me on the spot when she learns I planted the story that she and her kids had died in the explosion.*

He patted the newspaper article in his coat pocket. *Too bad. I—no, we—needed the cover. Yeah, right.*

Spanish moss hung in long finger-like tendrils from the trees that formed a canopy over the dark country road. The headlights sliced through the curtain of insects that filled the fermenting bayou air. He loved every sight, sound, and smell that came from the swamps. He'd spent most of his childhood here with his grandfather, who taught him its secrets. A wonderful place to grow up in and a wonderful place to come home to. After this job, he'd return to stay for the rest of his life.

If he survived.

Deep in thought, he suddenly swerved to avoid the splotch of white in the middle of the road. Bringing the car to a halt, he got out to examine what he'd almost run over. A tiny fur ball meowed up to him. As if asking for help, it held out an injured paw. Scooping up the kitten, he gingerly placed it on the front seat beside him. No use leaving it to become some alligator's next snack.

He could just hear his aunt, Evangeline, saying, "What's one more thing to take care of?" She hadn't minded staying with KC's kids and had even brought along her old mutt Harley, to keep them company. Aunt E never questioned him about anything. She just jumped in, taking care of whatever, whenever, just as she'd taken care of him, half raising him along with her own children. When his grandfather had been killed during a traffic stop, it was Aunt E who'd kept him from going over the edge.

Janko turned left onto a dirt path, drove fifty feet and stopped, turning off the car lights. In the rear view mirror, he watched the small amount of dust he'd made dissolve into the bayou mist. He knew he hadn't been followed, but had to make sure.

The night sounds closed in around him. In the distance he heard an alligator barking, and closer, tree frogs sang in syncopation with whippoorwills, the hum of the insects pelting the car, and the gentle lapping of water. He'd pity anyone stupid enough to get lost in the bayou. If gators or snakes didn't get 'em, insects or suffocating black water would.

The kitten crawled into his lap, still favoring its tiny paw. As Janko scratched behind its ears, he only hoped that KC's kids, like the cat, would turn to him for comfort, and not see him as the enemy.

What were their names? Ashley and Tyler, yeah, that's right. It'd been cruel to separate them from their mother, but so damn easy. Too easy.

Convinced that he hadn't been followed, he started the engine once more. After another half mile, the dirt road turned into an oyster-shell driveway that glowed white under the moonlight. The tires crunched noisily as he drove slowly up to the old house. Huge live oaks, their limbs swept low to the ground, stood like guardians just as they had before the Civil War.

Home. His private sanctuary where he escaped, where he could bury himself in another time when his life was good, right and pure. He shook his head as the irony of the situation struck him hard. He'd never trusted KC enough to bring her home, but it was the first place he'd thought of—and the safest—to bring her kids.

With the kitten in hand, he climbed the broad front steps, then stopped at the door. He hadn't called Aunt E to tell her he was coming, and knowing her, he could find himself on the wrong end of the shotgun kept in the hall tree by the front door. It wasn't Aunt E and the shotgun that he worried him, but the kids. What would be their reaction to seeing him again? Fear? Hatred? Shaking his head in resignation, he knew there was no use putting off the inevitable.

He walked into the foyer, where the sounds of laughter made him halt. It wasn't what he'd expected as he listened to the three voices. It'd been too damn long since this house had been filled with life.

"Aunt E, I'm home.

Harley, his big paws sounding like thunder on the wood floor, came bounding in, followed by Tyler, Aunt E, and then Ashley.

His aunt's face lined with concern. "*Mon p'tit*, what are you doing here?"

"I know you! You're that man—"

"Shut up, Tyler." Ashley pulled her brother back by the collar of his T-shirt, then protectively wrapped her arms around him.

Aunt E put her hand on Ashley's shoulder. "Everything is fine, *cherie*. This is his house, and I'm sure he'll explain. Won't you?" Her gaze pinned him firmly in place.

"Yes, I will. After you get this beast off me." Harley, his paws on Janko's shoulders, was giving the objecting kitten a tongue bath.

"C'm here, boy," Tyler called good naturedly.

"What have you brought home now?" Aunt E held out her hand as Janko released custody of his charge. "Why it's a tiny *chaton*."

"It has a hurt paw." His words sounded moronic, but he couldn't think of anything else to say as he was bombarded by the anger radiating from Ashley. If looks could kill, he'd be dead where he stood. She truly was her mother's daughter.

"Let's go into the kitchen and see what we can do to patch this sweet thing."

Leave it up to Aunt E to know how to diffuse a tense situation. They followed, watching as she placed the kitten on the large butcher-block island and examined the paw. "It's not broken, just bruised. Where did you get it?"

"Found it on the road not far from here." He gestured with his head in the direction of the road.

"Some uncarin' person just dumped it. Probably the whole litter and this is the only one to survive. See..." Aunt E cradled the kitten in one hand, then gently rolled it so all four paws were in the air. "...the pads have scratches all over. But, with a little rest and some good food, she'll be good as new." She put the tiny fur ball down, and it wobbled over to Ashley. "Looks like she knows where a good home be."

Ashley scooped it to her chest.

"What are you going to name her?" Janko spoke softly. Their gazes locked fractionally before she put the kitten down.

"You name it. I already have a cat." A bored look slid into her deep blue eyes.

"Yes, I know." He didn't really, but he had to take a chance to find a connection with these kids. KC had always wanted one—lots of animals, not just cats and dogs—but they'd never been able to with their unpredictable schedule.

Tyler, who'd been quiet up till then, shot out questions faster than a machine gun. "How do you know Ash has a cat? Have you been to our house? Do you know my dad? Do you know that I have a dog and my own horse? Why are we here? When are we going home? How come you didn't come with us on that plane? Is this really your house?"

"Whoa there, Slick, one question at a time." Janko couldn't help grinning at the boy as he reached out to tousle the thick blond hair.

"Mother calls Ty 'Slick' sometimes. Do you even know our mother?" Ashley stood with her arms locked across her chest, looking every bit the typical angry teenager.

"Yes, I know her quite well." He raised one eyebrow. "We worked together a long time ago.

"Wow, that's cool. My mom used to work? What'd she do?" Tyler's eyes shone with excitement. "I never knew she did anything other than be a mom, and train horses."

Janko's laughter filled the kitchen. "I'll tell you about it sometime. Right now, shouldn't y'all be getting ready for bed? It's past eleven, and I don't know about you, but I'm exhausted."

"Come on, *chers*, off to bed and in the morning he will still be here. Aunt E shepherded the kids up the back stairs, leaving him alone in the kitchen with the kitten.

****

After a restless night, Janko awakened before the sun broke through the trees. What exactly was he going to tell KC's kids? Certainly not the truth, but he had to say something to them. He gritted his teeth as he walked to his closet, pulling out some clothes. His ability to concoct believable covers, or to design and implement clandestine operations was the best in the world, yet the thought of facing her kids filled him with doubt and anxiety. Hell, he was just plain worried. Kids could see right through crap. So, whatever he told them, he'd better make it good.

Dressed in faded jeans and a T-shirt, he followed the

aroma of chicory into the kitchen. His aunt, already dressed, sat on a barstool, watching the kitten devour scraps of ham.

"Morning, Aunt E. You're up early." He kissed her leathery cheek.

"Got to have my morning time. Sleep well?" She didn't wait for his answer. "I've known you your whole life, *mon p'tit*, so what's going on? You've brought into your home two scared children, although Tyler bluffs just like you did. And that girl..."

Aunt E's mixture of English and Cajun flew out faster than he could absorb, but her meaning was clear. She liked KC's kids. He poured a tall mug of the thick brew for himself and refilled Aunt E's. "They were in danger. I had to make sure they were safe while their mother works with me on one last mission." He ran his fingers through his hair, then turned on a stove burner to light a cigarette.

"Non! Not in the house. Not around those *chers*." She wagged a finger at him. "I wish you'd stop that nasty habit."

He turned off the burner, snapped the cigarette in half, then tossed it in the trash. Taking a sip of his coffee, he closed his eyes as he savored the robust liquid for a moment. "Did Flavia have any problems with the kids?"

Aunt E guffawed. "Surely, you jest. You know she can charm a snake outta his fangs, and have him beg her to take his eyes too." She beamed with unabashed pride. "It was good to see my baby girl, even for a few minutes. You really must have something going."

"The less you know, the safer we'll be. If something should happen, you still remember what to do?"

She nodded as she stared out the bay window into the rose garden. "Head for the swamp to my Zeke's, then on to Granny's cabin on Black Bayou."

Without a word, he crossed over to Aunt E and wrapped her in a hug. *God, it was good to be home. No need to pretend. No need to explain. No need to justify, rectify, or sanctify.*

He didn't let go until he heard the footsteps in the dining room. Tyler pushed the swinging door so hard it banged against the counter.

"Geez, this ol' house is so big, I get lost every time I turn around. What's for breakfast?"

"How about good morning to us first?" Janko looked down sternly. He wasn't used to kids disrupting his morning, or for that matter disrupting his life.

"Oh, yeah, sorry. Good morning Aunt E. Morning...what *am* I supposed to call you?" The boy's face squinched in confusion.

"What would you like to call me? Uncle Steve?"

"Nah, you're not really my uncle. Lemme think a minute."

"Most people just call me Janko."

"That sounds dorky. What does Mom call you?"

What names hadn't KC called him in the years they'd known each other? None that he'd tell her twelve-year-old son. "Well, you can decide what you'd like best."

"Cool. G'morning to you, sir. Now, what's for breakfast?"

The kid had a one-track mind, and an empty stomach. Had he been like that? "Where's your sister?

"That big baby. She cried most of the night, and she's still bawling this morning. I told her to think of this like Mom would—'an adventure to be explored.' That just made her cry harder. Stupid girls."

He turned his attention from Janko to Aunt E. "I know how to make pancakes, if you show me where the stuff is. My mom taught me 'n Ash how to take care of ourselves, in case we got hungry and she had to be outside.

His dark brown eyes somberly conveyed his good intentions. As Janko watched Tyler place his hand in Aunt E's to help her from the stool, he could see a lot of KC in him. *Guess he's all right, for a kid.*

"Aunt E, I'll go see about Ashley, if you can help Slick

here get breakfast started for us." Janko refilled his mug before taking the back stairs two at a time.

As he neared the room that was once his sister's, he heard soft sobs. He stood quietly in the hall looking in. Sarah's room was still the way she'd left it when she married Phillip years ago. If life had been fair, it would have been her daughter's. Or his even his. If he had wanted kids.

The soft whir of the ceiling fan fluttered the white lace curtains framing the French doors that led out to the balcony. The wallpaper with the tiny yellow roses made the room seem like an indoor version of the rose garden below. The white iron bed and white furniture trimmed in gold rested on an oak floor that bore the scars of a hundred and fifty years of living. Ashley's well-worn Nikes lying on the Persian rug were the only reminder that Sarah wasn't here. She'd never left anything out of its assigned place.

He rapped twice on the doorframe. "May I come in?"

"Go away! You're the cause of all of this." Ashley pulled her pillow on top of her head.

"I'm not going away. You can talk to me now, or you can talk to me later. I'll be right here, either way." Leaning against the jamb, he waited for her to see if he'd gone. He didn't have to wait long. "You know, you're so much like my sister, it's scary. She used to do the same thing, but I could outlast her, so you might as well let me have my way."

Her groan, muffled by the pillow, let him know he'd won. He stopped the grin from forming. "Your mother is fine, if that helps. She knows you're safe." That was another lie, but he'd tell KC as soon as he saw her.

Ashley pushed the pillow down to her stomach, then pulled the comforter under her chin. "Why are you doing this to us? I want to go home." He detected a tremor in her voice.

"You and your brother needed a secure place to stay for awhile. Your mother didn't have time to tell you, but she'll explain it all when you see her." *If we get out of this alive.*

"But why couldn't we have gone to Randy's? Does he even know where we are?" Tears pooled in the corners of her eyes.

Janko rubbed the stubble on his chin, "No, he doesn't know—"

"I don't want to be here. You're holding Tyler and me against our will, and that's kidnapping. She clutched the comforter, but her head remained high, her gaze fastened on his.

What could he tell her but the truth? She was much too smart to be fooled, and if he got caught lying to her now, there'd be no chance to build any kind of trust. "You're right, Ashley. I did sorta kidnap you and your brother." He ran his fingers through his hair. This was harder than he'd anticipated.

"The reasons you're here right now aren't important. What is, is that you listen and follow the instructions I'm leaving with you and Aunt E. Not only for your safety, but for your mother's." He'd gotten her full attention with that last bit. "After breakfast, you and Tyler are going to make a videotape."

"Are we supposed to ask for a ransom, or are you going to?" Ashley spat sarcastically at him as she sat up straight.

"No, nothing that melodramatic. I wanted to give you a chance to let your mom know that you're okay. She's concerned about you." As Ashley slumped against the pillows, he slowly exhaled.

All his life he'd been able to read people, but this time, he wasn't sure if he'd made an ally or an enemy. The girl was so much like her mother, yet so different, too. He paused a moment, but when she didn't respond, he turned to leave. "Tyler and Aunt E are making pancakes for breakfast," he said over his shoulder. "Join us if you want to. Go hungry if you don't."

****

Kelly's alarm clock blared, bringing with it the realization that every muscle in her body hurt. It even hurt to breathe. Time had tap-danced on her with metal cleats and she felt each puncture. Murph had been wrong about her shape reverting back to its youthful form in no time. This was going to be a long and painful day, but she'd lived through worse. She couldn't dwell on the physical. She had to focus strictly on what she had to do to get her children back. Every day without them was torture far worse than the soreness in her body.

Wherever Janko had taken them, could he keep them out of danger while she was gone? God help him if he didn't! She'd kill him for sure.

Her fourth day of training began early, as had the previous three, with running the obstacle course. Today, she'd master "the damn Wall" no matter how many times she had to try. She pictured herself running up to the ten-foot wall, grabbing the rope, pulling herself up high enough to reach the top and going over. Before starting, she stretched her taut muscles, a small smile parted her lips as she could almost see Tyler beside her teasing her for acting so old, and slow. He could have outlasted them all and taught her a few tricks, especially the wall rope. So many times she'd watched him scamper up the hay pulley into the rafters of the barn, then with a mighty Tarzan yell, swing down to terrorize any hapless human, beast or fowl lingering too long in the broad hallway.

Once on the course, she zipped through the first two obstacles, then jogged down the trail. A twinge in her side made her gasp. The old scar pulled as she extended her legs farther and faster. Janko told her she'd gotten too comfortable, and he'd been right. She'd lost her edge and failed those she loved the most. Her complacency had cost her too much, and that would haunt her forever.

As she ran, she replayed her last conversation with Ashley, her miracle baby who'd saved her sanity after Janko had punched a hole in the wall of her life.

"Mom, please take me into town to get my ears

pierced again. All the girls in my group have theirs already."

"I've got too much to do today with the party tonight, but maybe Friday. Could we agree on that?"

"Ah Mom, Friday will never get here."

Damn it, why didn't I do what she wanted? Will I ever get to...Stop it.

Sweat ran into her eyes, camouflaging the tears zigzagging down her cheeks. There was no way that she'd break stride to wipe away any evidence of her weakness. Even the sun's burning rays couldn't slow her. Her mind had to become calloused, even though her legs threatened mutiny as she pushed the ground harder. No surrender. No mercy, not even for herself. She couldn't allow anything to distract her from her mission.

"KC..."

Dread shimmied up her spine and she clenched her jaw, recognizing the voice that had haunted her innermost being. She quickened her pace on the trail. This was not the time or place that she wanted to see Janko. She wasn't ready, but then she'd never be ready until he returned her kids.

"KC, wait!"

He was closer. She could hear his footfalls now and knew he'd catch her, but she'd make him work at it. "Well, hell, Janko, get your lazy ass up here. You're slowing me down." Wasn't it just like him to begin the course at the halfway point?

"Murphy tells me you're pushing too hard." He matched her stride.

"I've got a lot of catching up to do."

"KC, you're no good to me hurt. While I need you in top form, an injury at this point will delay our mission." His blue eyes pierced hers. Chips from a glacier were warmer.

She spun him around by one arm. "That's right, Janko, it's always the company first. You have your priorities and I have mine." Dropping his arm, she sprinted a few feet away. "I'm working again for only one reason—you kidnapped my children. You have no clue what life is really all about and what's important in this world. People. Relationships. But you wouldn't know about that, would you? How does that cold empty bed feel now?"

Waves of fury radiated through her as she attacked the Wall and scaled it before he could grab the rope. She was proud to say that she made it over the first time, and she used the same anger to propel herself at top speed over the giant web of ropes and across the water pit pole. She thought she could hear him, but when she glanced back, there was no one behind her.

Damn him. A part of her was glad she'd lost him and another mad because the sight of him made her guts tighten into knots. The wind cooled her as she flew down the high wire, landing on her feet, and started on the final run back to the barracks.

Just a few more minutes and a hot shower will be mine, then I'll ask Murph to...

A flash of white was all she saw before the impact sent her flying. Janko attacked her from behind a small wall of shrubbery. As she fought to refill her depleted lungs, instinct took over. The will to survive—the need to win—controlled her, but he was too strong, and her muscles were too sore.

How many times had she passed these bushes and never thought about an ambush? Ambush—the irony of the word.

"Caught you napping, didn't I?" Janko pinned her arms above her head, the scent of pine surrounding them. "The KC I trained wouldn't have allowed that to happen." His crisp T-shirt remained snowy white and sweat-free, unlike hers.

She breathed in short gulps, unable to hurl the insults that welled inside her. *Relax, relax. All you have to use is what is inside you.*

Seeing him this close—mere inches away—and

feeling the familiar weight of his body pressing her down still hurt, even after so many years. A few more lines framed his eyes, and gray streaked his much shorter hair and moustache. He was as devastatingly handsome as the day she'd met him.

When she was twenty-one, he'd intrigued her. By twenty-four, she'd fallen in love with him. One short year later, he'd taught her to trust no one, most especially him.

Finally able to take a full breath, she couldn't resist a few verbal jabs. "I see that time has added a few gray hairs to your mane. Thinking about using color? A lot of men do. At least, you haven't lost much." If there had been one vanity about him, it was his hair. She grinned as his eyes turned flinty and he ground her hips deeper into the soft earth. "Oh ho, so did I hit a nerve?"

"Good try, KC, but not this time. He flashed a smile that showed even, white teeth as he lowered himself until she bore his full weight now.

For a brief moment, she thought he was going to kiss her. Like molten lava finding a tiny crack, her anger spread through her, strengthening her tired muscles. She tossed him on his side and quickly brought her knee up, only to find her leg scissored between his. He rolled, forcing her to follow or risk injury to her knee.

She moved with him, not finished by half.

Her hand crept down into her fatigue pocket where her fingers curled around a knife. She slowly slid it free, opening the blade with her thumb. The sun glinted off the steel blinding him momentarily before the deadly sharp edge rested gently against his throat.

He made no move to protect or defend himself.

"Damn, babe, it feels dull."

Kelly slowly pulled the knife toward her, leaving a dotted line of blood. "Don't play games with me, Steven. If you didn't have my children hidden God only knows where, I'd slit your throat without another thought." She flicked her wrist, throwing the blade into the small triangle created between his legs and hers. Her gaze followed his to the quivering black handle. "Have I made my point?"

"Most definitely, KC dear. Loud and clear." Untangling his legs, he got to his feet.

He'd never before stared at her like that. Was it disappointment she read in his face? What had he expected, that she would greet him with open arms? That her hatred, still so intense after all these years, would be lessened because he had her children? She watched him brush off his clothes, tucking in his T-shirt as he started toward the barracks.

A piece of newspaper wafted to the ground. "Hey, you're getting sloppy in your old age. You dropped something." She bent to retrieve both her knife and the paper. The wind caught the edges of the clipping, flipping it over so she could read the headlines. The knife fell from her limp hand.

THE DAILY OKLAHOMAN

Treaty Hill, Oklahoma—Tragedy struck this small farming community early Tuesday morning when a house exploded at the residence of Kelly C. Wood. Ms. Wood, 39, and her two children, Ashley, 14 and Tyler, 12 were killed by the blast. Local officials ruled it accidental due to a natural gas leak.

Private services will be held for the immediate family, according to Randall Wood, the children's father, and Ms. Wood's ex-husband.

Shock doused her like a bucket of ice water as she stared at the picture of her leveled house. *Oh God, how could this be true? Randy's parents, they must be devastated. Our neighbors. Our friends. How horrible. The animals, my horses, are they all right?*

Rational thoughts began to come to her. There couldn't have been a gas leak. She'd just had an annual inspection of the whole house. Someone destroyed it! If she hadn't left the night before...if Janko hadn't taken the children from school...my God, they could all really be dead!

But, wait a minute. Randy knew the kids weren't there. They'd fought before she'd left, so why was he going along with this? What the hell was going on?

All her pent up rage and frustration manifested in her scream. "Steven!" She caught up to him, her hand shaking as she held out the newspaper. "What's happening? Who did this?"

He regarded her calmly, his face impassive except for the twitch of a jaw muscle. "The game has changed. The hunter now becomes the hunted. Are you surprised? They know who you are and where you live—lived."

Taking several deep breaths, she steadied her nerves. "My kids, I've got to make sure they're all right." She needed more than just to see them, she needed to hold them, to reassure them—and herself. "What if they see this? They won't understand! Grabbing his arm, her resolve slipped as tears filled her eyes. "I'll do anything you want, I'll... Please let me see them."

"Have you lost your fuckin' mind?" he said coldly. "Do you honestly think I'm going to put them, and us, at risk by taking you to see them?" He turned his head away, his gaze not meeting hers.

He was right, and she knew it. She hadn't been thinking as an agent, but reacting as a mother. Had she really gotten so soft? What could she say to him that would make him understand the terror she was experiencing right now? He'd never understand. He couldn't, because he'd never raised a child.

"It's time to go, KC."

Yes, she agreed as her resolve hardened. She couldn't—wouldn't—go back to a life looking over her shoulder. Someone was after her and her children, and they'd never be safe until that someone was dead.

Yes, it *was* time to go.

Time to kill the threat to her family.

She would take great satisfaction in doing so.

Chapter Four

Saying good-bye to Murphy was harder than she'd expected. They'd grown close again in the few days she'd been there, and right now, she wanted to blurt out what Janko told her, as if telling Murphy could make sense of this devastating turn of events. But nothing made sense anymore, so she kept her thoughts and fears to herself.

"Good luck to you, lass. I know you'll be seeing your children in no time." The grizzled old man had tears in his eyes as he hugged her tightly.

She couldn't shake the feeling she wasn't in top form and didn't want to leave the safety of the base. It had been such a long time since she'd had to use all her skills. Had she made herself good again? Good enough to gamble with her life, and the lives her of children? They were depending on her to finish this. Murphy's arms loosened and she stepped back, memorizing the details of his face just in case she never saw him again. Her footsteps rang hollow as she walked down the long dark hallway.

Outside, she spotted Sarge standing ramrod straight as he waited next to the same Jeep that had brought her to the ramshackle base. The same mirrored sunglasses, the same stony face, the same condescending attitude. I've made his day by leaving, she thought as she slammed her bags in the back of the Jeep, then climbed into the passenger seat and crossed her arms.

Janko jumped in. "Let's go."

The silent drive was soon broken by the sound of a jet engine. The same plane waited, but this time no agents flanked the open staircase.

Sarge stopped her as she reached for her bag. "No mercy."

His words startled her. *No mercy.* For Janko's mission, or herself? His mission would come off without a hitch. And she could kill the target without a second thought, without remorse. As for herself, she didn't deserve any.

Taking her bag, she walked to the jet, then turned at the top of the stairs for one last look, stunned when Sarge saluted her. A chill ran through her as she nodded in return. The specter of self-doubt that had haunted her was now replaced with an inner strength born of confidence. With that one tiny gesture from someone who'd only known her for a few days, she knew she was going to succeed.

She took a few steps inside. The rows of windows flooded the plane's interior with sunlight. There was nothing she hadn't seen before, but now it all seemed so different. Janko was seated at the table, shuffling papers, looking relaxed in his navy Dockers and white golf shirt. She was anything but calm, jumping when someone closed the hatch behind her.

"You aren't piloting the plane?" she growled as she searched for a place to put her bag, then finally dropped it at the end of the couch.

"No." He snapped on the intercom, "We're ready to take off."

Dammit! She'd counted on spending the flight time to wherever alone instead of with him, or worse, near him. Flopping down into a chair, she turned her back to him; perhaps he'd get the hint and disappear.

The engines raced briefly before the plane began moving down the runway. Her attention was drawn out the window where she watched the jet's shadow darken the brush, then the tall line of trees as they went airborne until only blue sky remained. Every minute brought her closer to the job she had to do, but her thoughts turned to her children. She missed them so. If Janko hadn't taken them... she flattened her hand against her thigh, as if that simple act could stop the tears that stung her eyes.

****

Janko studied KC's profile. She still had it all—beauty, brains, balls. Sending her away fifteen years ago had been like severing a piece of himself. Necessary, but it hurt like hell. He'd let her too far inside. They'd been so close they could almost read each other's minds. Although her face showed no emotion, he knew now that she was battling to control the anguish she was trying so hard to hide. And she was losing.

Hell fire! I need her focused, in sync with the job we have to do. Just like it used to be. He rose from the table and walked to a cabinet, pulling harder than was necessary on the gear bag stowed inside, and ground his teeth at the sound of ripping fabric. Returning to the table, he took out a battery-operated VCR, the size of a small laptop computer. After raising the monitor, he slid the unit toward her. Maybe this would help. He had nothing to lose. She was worthless to him like this, and it would be better to find out now if she could pull herself together than to learn she couldn't out in the field.

"Hiya, Mom!" The boy's voice boomed.

Janko knew he'd done the right thing when he saw her shoulders relax. The worry lines faded from her eyes as a few tears escaped down her cheeks. Her hands trembled as she reached to touch the image on the screen. The tape ended with both kids reassuring her they were fine and not to worry about them.

Was that gratitude in the look she'd just given him? He closed the monitor and started to put the machine away when she put her hand on his, stopping him.

"Give me a minute," she whispered as the tape rewound.

He'd give her a minute, an hour, the whole damn day, if that was what she needed. The tape had been fun to make, that is, after he'd convinced Ashley to do it. He'd put Tyler in charge of setting up the equipment. The boy was fascinated by watching himself on TV as the tape rolled. Ashley had used her time on-camera discreetly trying to tell her mother where they were. Janko had kept his laughter corked, pretending he didn't realize what she was doing, but he had to hand it to her, she was one smart kid.

KC released the unit to him. "I know I should say 'Thank you,' but why couldn't you have taken me to them? You took the risk once, why not again?"

Because I'm a bastard. Because I couldn't take the chance you'd vanish with the kids.

Because I couldn't trust you.

He watched her take a deep breath, then another, as he put the machine back in the bag and placed it on the floor.

"Janko, I'm going renegade."

"You can't." He kept his voice low and even.

"Who the hell are you to tell me I can't?" She leapt from her chair, and for a split second, he thought she was going for his throat. But she stopped mere inches from where he sat. Her stare, just short of feral, made him feel as if he were a helpless rat, trapped with no way out.

"You're working for me." He slowly rose.

"I don't care what *your* mission is, but I promise I'll help you after I kill the bastard who's threatening my family. Explain to Control for me."

"I can't."

"*Can't* or won't? Explain to Control or let me go solo?"

She stood mere inches away from him, looking like she was ready to go *Cujo*. He dreaded telling her he'd lied about this mission and was lying about other things as well. Ever since Osprey, he'd lied to her, to Control, and most of all, to himself. But no more.

When she grabbed his arm, her fingernails bit into his flesh. "Tell me now!"

"We're on our own. No back up. Nothing." She couldn't have looked more stunned if he'd slapped her.

"Control doesn't *know?* Your mission isn't agency sanctioned?"

"No."

"Then how—"

"Because my mission is *you*. The threat against you has come from inside Pegasus. You're the target, the mark. You're the one they want."

"Why me? Huh? Why now after fifteen years?" Her fist hitting his chest punctuated each word.

He looked down, noticing crescents of blood where her nails had been. The throb in his arm spread to a dull ache behind his eyes. He sat and cradled his head between his hands, his index fingers rubbing the bridge of his nose. Even with his eyes closed, he could feel her gaze raking over him. Now was the time to tell her everything. "Sit down."

"No!"

Opening his eyes, he caught the flash of anger in hers. He rested his hands on the table, then paused to prepare what he had to say. "Early Monday morning I discovered that you and your kids were in danger."

"Why didn't you call me? I could have—"

"Would you have believed me?" Her silence told him what he already knew, that she would never trust him again. He'd betrayed her too many times. It shouldn't have hurt, but, oh God, it did. He continued, his voice devoid of emotion, "Cheryl Paxton—"

"Who's Cheryl?" KC knitted her eyebrows.

"Security Specialist, a good one."

"Yeah, I'll bet." He didn't miss her sarcasm.

"She came into my office after intercepting a coded message for Carl Delacourt—"

"Carl Delacourt?" She towered over him, the heat radiating from her seared his skin.

"She knew he was no longer black-ops scheduled, and he'd called in sick earlier, so she brought it to me. I read it then went through his desk—"

"Wasn't his office locked?"

"Are you going to keep interrupting me?" Janko glared at her. "When has any lock ever stopped me? As chief of operations, it's my job to know what's going on, and you should be *damned* glad."

"Yeah, yeah. Who sent the message?" She slipped into the chair next to him. Her fingernails tapped a staccato beat while he pulled a paper from his briefcase, then tossed it toward her.

"If I knew that, don't you think I'd have taken care of the situation without involving you?" His cynicism was wasted on her as she began to read the message aloud.

"'Retrieve Glock 39 with 14 round mag in OKC. Dispose excess.'"

She pushed it back. "A Glock 39 is a 45 caliber, not a 9mm, and the magazine holds only six bullets, not fourteen. That message doesn't even make sense. So what does it have to do with me?"

"How old are you and how old is your daughter?" He scanned her face, watching her brief surge of anger flame out along with the color in her face. "OKC was the code on your file. You were the best special gun Pegasus ever had."

Her breath caught in her throat. She didn't need any further explanation. "They were planning to take Ashley and me, then kill Tyler. *Why?*" She turned deathly white, grasping the chair arms as if she was about to collapse.

"I don't know." He reached across the table and placed his hand on her shoulder, only to have her shake it off, then look at him. The sight of her eyes brimming with unshed tears tore at his heart.

"My files were sealed. Murphy said *he* couldn't even find me, so how...?"

Janko gave a short derisive laugh. "I don't know." *I've known where you were since the day I sent you away.*

She rose unsteadily, walked to one of the windows, then stood with her arms wrapped around her middle. He'd seen her do this only twice in all the times they'd been together, at her mother's funeral and when she'd been forced out of Pegasus. Her body trembled as if she was cold inside and out. He started to follow her, but forced himself to stay seated. The immense desire to enfold her shaking body tightly against his and whisper that everything was going to be okay was so strong, it almost won out. But logically, he couldn't give her that assurance. Nothing was certain anymore except the safety of her children. So he would wait.

Wait until she came to him.

Shaking out a cigarette, he lit it and watched the smoke form a cloud on the ceiling. It hovered for a moment, then the circulating air caught and dragged it into a thin line before making it disappear. Smoke and shadows. There one minute, gone the next. He'd lived that way most of his life. It'd kept him from getting killed, from entanglements, from loving. If he wasn't careful, he'd find himself doing more than simply wanting to protect KC. And that wouldn't be good for either of them.

Kelly squared her shoulders and clenched her hands in an effort to make the numbness go away. Her temples now pounded as if all her blood were centering there. A threat from inside the agency? Why after all this time had passed? Why Ashley? What if Janko hadn't been there? She could find no answers to the questions haunting her. "What do we do now?" she whispered, her back still turned to him.

"We go after Delacourt."

She whirled around to confront him. "And how do you propose to do that? You've cut us off from our assets. Tied our hands, forced us so deep undercover—"

"I know where the bastard is." She waited as he took another drag off his cigarette, then stubbed it out. With the butt, he traced a pattern in the ashtray before he finally glanced her way. "Austin."

It was a cruel twist of fate to return to the city where her new life with Janko had begun. Where she'd been so naïve. Where she'd loved him. She snorted scornfully. "Why Austin?"

"Because that's where he planned to take you—"

"Let me take a wild guess about what's next. You need me to flush him out, right?"

Janko shifted nervously in his chair and reached for another Marlboro. Her hand came down quickly on his, stopping him, then she snatched the pack away. "It's time to quit. At least around me."

"Sure, no problem," he said smugly.

"Yeah, right." She hurled the pack at him, and he caught it one handed in mid-air.

"Thanks," he said, his expression turning sober. "I can't do this without you."

"Why? Because I'm the one he wants? Because you don't want to kill a friend?"

"No." Now it was his turn to pace as she'd done earlier. She watched as his fingers raked through his hair. "Because I need you with me."

She opened her mouth, then shut it when a biting retort just wouldn't come. He'd never admitted to her before that he *needed* her—not even during the deadliest of missions. This was as foreign to her as the fact that someone was after her. Could she trust him? But, *how?* She'd done it before, and he'd let her down. That had almost destroyed her. Besides, she'd been on her own for so long and she'd done all right... except for a lousy marriage, and letting her kids get snatched, and not protecting them...

No, she couldn't risk another betrayal. But Janko had revealed a tiny flaw in his armor. He needed her. Or was this his way to sucker her in, only to tear her down? She couldn't allow him to hurt her again.

She had to escape, to think clearly, to weigh her options. A tight scowl formed on her face. *What* options? She had none. It was either trust Janko and work together as a team, or go it alone and monumentally increase her risk of falling into Delacourt's hands.

Ah, hell! She could die either way, but she didn't plan on dying soon—and sure as hell didn't plan on dying alone. There wasn't much of a decision to make. If she wanted her kids back, and any chance at a normal life, she had no choice but to trust Janko.

He knew it, too. He'd tossed the dice, betting their lives on her, and he'd won this roll. And the next one? They would either come out winners or losers, and she'd come too far to be a loser now. A half growl, half groan of resignation escaped her. She'd go along with him, but would reserve judgment on how much she would trust him. One false move, one more lie, one hint that he wasn't on the up and up, it would be over, and she'd be gone.

The tension between them was broken by the plane's change in altitude. She sat on the couch and looked out the window. A thrill of excitement eased the heaviness inside her. Her heartbeat quickened, as it always did when she first saw the terrain change from prairie flatness to soft rolling hills of white limestone dotted with scrub cedars. The Hill Country of Texas was home. A small part of her wished they could stay up longer so she could see the Highland lakes from the air.

A brief fly-over showed her how much Austin had grown since she'd graduated from the University of Texas. She didn't recognize the private airstrip they had landed on, or even what part of town they were in. Talk about shaking her up in a paper bag then letting her go. Gathering her few things, she stepped out of the plane onto the tarmac. The bright spring sunshine warmed her. She longed to smell the bluebonnets and Indian paintbrush that colored the field surrounding the runway.

He walked toward the terminal and she followed him part of the way, pausing in the shade of the oblong building. Her stomach rumbled, but she wasn't hungry. Allowing her bag to slide to the ground, she heard it land with a muffled thunk. She knelt beside it, absently toying with the nylon strap. What would her cover be? Was she going to even have a cover? She knew he had a plan, he always had a plan, and a plan B, C, D, but since he hadn't spoken another word to her, she was still as clueless as when she'd stepped on the plane.

****

Janko drove up alongside her, but she remained there in the shade, deep in thought. He wondered if she was remembering when they'd been everything to each other—partner, best friend, lover. It had been the best times of his life. When it had ended so badly, he'd sworn he would never let himself care that much again. But here he was, partnered with her again. Wanting her again. Feeling again. That was no damn good.

He stepped from the car, then cleared his throat to get her attention before holding out his hand to help her up. She grasped it and murmured a soft "Thank you." Their bodies brushed together, then she stepped back, pulling her hand free of his to grab her bag and toss it into the trunk next to his. His hand was still warm from her touch. He regretted letting it go.

"Ready?"

"As I'll ever be." She climbed in the passenger seat and shut the door. Her seat belt was fastened by the time he put the car in gear.

They drove toward the center of town in silence until she spotted The Tower, one of Austin's most recognizable landmarks.

"Hook 'Em Horns," she said with a grin, saluting the giant limestone structure.

"You do that in some cities, and it's a gang sign." He raised his index and pinkie then crossed his thumb over his bent middle and ring fingers. It did in some strange way look like a longhorn's head, except one horn was shorter than the other. He had a hard time understanding alumni fanaticism. His loyalty was to the school of hard knocks, and not the couple of colleges he'd dropped out of.

"Drive around campus for a moment."

He smiled faintly, pleased that she'd asked him for something. "My pleasure." From the wistful way she looked out the window, he'd bet she was visiting old ghosts, too.

He remembered the first time he saw her. Eighteen years ago he'd turned down the wrong corridor in the athletic building on the university campus. As much as he detested making mistakes, he'd never regretted watching that practice session of the Lady Longhorns. She'd caught his attention immediately, all legs and blond, just the way he liked his women. Her hair was in a tight braid that accented the refined structure of her face.

When he heard the girls leaving the building, he cut short his appointment with a fellow agent so he could see her one more time. Lounging against the wall, he watched as a knot of close-knit teammates walked past him. These were strong women, the kind who won championships because they knew how to play the game and come out on top. The tall blonde in the center exuded a self-confidence that screamed power. By damn, he loved a powerful woman. She'd make an excellent recruit, and he'd speculated...

Her hand on his arm brought him back to the present.

"There's the Drum."

He glanced over, noticing her eyes held a sparkle he hadn't seen in her in a long time, and she still had the inner strength that had enticed him so long ago.

"I loved playing basketball there." She smiled at him, and his chest tightened.

As if he could ever forget...

That night he sat in the stands where she could easily see him, not so hard given the attendance at women's sporting events. This was the fourth game he'd been to in the last two weeks. Kelly Carleen Garretty was exactly what he was looking for—smart, well educated, and alluring. Her ability to elude him after each game made her all the more fascinating. He'd run a preliminary background investigation, and Control had given him the thumbs up to bring her onboard. Tonight he'd speak to her, even if he had to follow her into the locker room.

The game started off with a typical Lady Longhorn

run, blowing by Southeastern University in the first ten minutes. She came in to relieve the post. From across the court, he heard her name yelled in a thick drawl just as she was about to release the ball, and her shot careened off the rim. Hustling, she yanked the ball from her opponent's hands, then went back up. The backboard shook as she slammed the ball home. Once again, her name could be heard echoing around the gym, but she never looked toward the man yelling at her. Janko began to pity the unfortunate girl assigned to guard her as she played with more intensity than he'd ever seen. With time running out in the first half, she stepped back across the three-point line, raised the ball to him in a salute, and let it fly. It touched the rim as the buzzer sounded. As the swish of the net reached his ear, she'd already disappeared into the tunnel.

During the second half, he moved a few rows behind the obnoxious screamer. For every shot she made or missed, a comment spewed from the man. Before the final buzzer, Janko had to leave before he strangled the guy, and missed his chance to talk to Kelly.

He approached her from a side corridor as she came out of the locker room, but stopped cold when she shook her head. Under the harsh florescent lights, he saw pain flicker once in her eyes before her face turned into a mask of stone. Puzzled, he peered around the corner as she passed by him to walk up to the screamer slouched against the tile wall. She dutifully tilted her cheek to him. Janko retreated into the shadows where he could still see and listen to their conversation.

"Hello, Father."

"Kelly, my angel," he slurred. "Aren't you happy to see your old dad?"

Even from a distance, Janko could tell that the man was drunk. He'd have to be the way he'd behaved in the stands and now, putting his hands all over his daughter. It made Janko sick to watch. Never would he call, or even think of her as, Kelly again. She surprised him when she took the keys from her father.

"Don't you want to come home for an early weekend? Your mother misses you."

She stared at him for a moment before she spoke hesitantly. "Oh, Father, I wish that I could, but—but I've got a big test. The professors do that so students can't sneak out before spring break."

"How 'bout I stay the night with you, Kel-ly? Your roommate left yesterday and you shouldn't really be alone." His arm went around her waist, pulling her in to him as they left the building.

Fury such as he'd never experienced before ate at Janko as he followed them outside. So that bastard was Patrick Garretty. His face was flaccid, the booze aging him far more than the photo Janko had found on the Internet. A protective instinct flared inside him. There was no way he was going to let her father near her tonight, or ever if he could help it. The tires on his black BMW slung gravel as he drove out of the parking lot. His lips pulled into an evil smirk. He would have a little surprise waiting for them, and have fun putting it into action.

With only minutes to spare, he reached her apartment, made short work of the lock and slipped inside. He heard her voice first, then her father's. Kelly's key slid into the lock, but before she could open the door, he flung it wide. If he'd only had a camera rolling to catch the way her mouth gaped open when she saw him standing half-naked in her apartment.

"Hey, babe, what took ya so long? I've been waiting, like, forever, you know, for you to get back. How was the game?" He pulled her against his bare chest, then kissed her possessively. Her lips were icy and she trembled. His finger hooked the belt loop on her jeans as he eased her to his left side.

Patrick Garretty's face turned maroon as waves of anger radiated from him, his red-rimmed eyes narrowed dangerously. Spittle flew from his lips, "Who—who is this?"

"Father, this is—"

"Oh wow, cool. I finally get to meet ya. Mark Stevens." Janko stuck out his right hand, all the time watching Patrick's malevolent gaze take in his disheveled appearance and partially zipped jeans. "Didn't you tell your parents about me at Christmas? Tsk, tsk. It's late, and—" he stretched, faking a yawn, "— I'm ready for bed. I'll just walk Pops back to his car to make sure he gets there safely."

"Whore." Patrick raised his fist near his daughter's face, then lowered it slightly before he stomped off.

Following him to the parking lot, Janko caught Patrick's arm, twisting it up and back, before throwing the surprised man across the hood of a car. He whispered, "I'm only going to say this once. I know who you are, what you are, and where I can find slime like you. Make one more minute of your daughter's life a nightmare, and you'll never wake up. If you understand, nod or something." He spun the old man around to face him.

"You son of a bitch! Bas—"

"Wrong answer, bucko." The chop to Patrick's throat swiftly cut off the remainder of the curses.

The sound of the blaring horn behind him brought him back to his surroundings. Austin certainly had changed since he and KC had left, and so had they. He drove down Congress Avenue toward the hotel. The setting sun reflected orange, gold and red off the tall glass buildings in the downtown area. Too bad the city had allowed the view of the Capitol to be obstructed.

And too bad he'd let his life become obstructed. Maybe after all of this was over? Nah, he could never love her, not the way a woman like her deserved to be loved. She didn't need him in her life. He would only bring her misery.

Pulling into the parking lot, he was past ready to check into their hotel, order room service and relax. Today had been long. Tomorrow would be even longer.

Chapter Five

KC snatched the key card from Janko's hand and fumbled with the lock. Knowing he was behind her—waiting, scrutinizing—frustrated her even further. Finally, the green light came on and she shoved open the door to be greeted by a blast of cold air scented with orange. She took a few cautious steps inside, surveying their accommodations.

The spacious suite had an overstuffed sofa upholstered in jewel tones against one wall, flanked by two freestanding brass lamps. The shiny coffee table, covered with a brocade runner, held the TV remote, with a few artfully arranged magazines. In the corner was a small glass top breakfast table with two plush chairs and a single carnation centerpiece. Sheer curtained patio doors opened to a spectacular view of Town Lake and the Congress Avenue Bridge. If it had been summer, she would be able to watch the Mexican Freetail bats fly out at dusk from under bridge. She continued on with her inspection of the room.

To her right was a kitchenette complete with sink, coffeepot, microwave and mini-fridge. Two coffee cups, along with creamer and sugar packets, lay nestled in a napkin lined wicker basket. A pottery bowl filled with fresh fruit was on the bar that separated the two areas.

On the other side of the room a set of curtained French doors piqued her curiosity enough to walk across the plush emerald carpet. Grabbing both curved brass handles, she threw wide the doors, finding the room flooded with natural light from the floor to ceiling window and dominated by the biggest bed she'd ever seen.

"Wow! Wonder what your room looks like?" She ran her hand across the silky bedspread. This would almost make up for the nights spent on the cot at the base.

"This is my room," he said dryly.

"Like hell it is." She glanced over her shoulder at him. His face displayed no emotion and she knew he was serious. Fine. Shrugging, she looked back at the bed. "Enjoy the couch, Slick, 'cuz you're not sleeping in here."

Everything seemed surreal. Here she was in Austin, Texas, hunting a maniac when she should be in Treaty Hill, Oklahoma, watching her kids play ball or competing in a rodeo play day. And most assuredly, she should not be here with Janko. She shook her head. Monday morning had started out so normally, and now, Friday afternoon, her life was anything but.

The adrenaline that had kept her moving all day deserted her and she couldn't remember a time when she'd been this bone-tired weary. Dropping her bag on the floor, she grabbed a couple of pillows and the remote and tossed them on the end of the bed before she belly flopped down.

She ignored Janko until he moved in front of the TV. "We have some work to do."

The irritation in his voice hit a nerve. "Yeah, right. How much work does the piece of cheese do on the mouse trap?" she asked flippantly as she aimed the remote around him, trying to get it to work.

"I'm serious, KC. I'll order us some lunch and we'll work out our operational plan." He waited for an answer she didn't want to give.

At long last she nodded, then from the corner of her eye she watched him walk away. He wasn't going to give her any peace, but then their relationship had never been tranquil.

The bed had now lost its comfortableness, so she rolled off, slid back the patio door, and stepped onto the balcony. A small puff of wind lifted a wisp of hair, depositing it in her face. She tucked it behind her ear, then stared out at the lake, watching a lone sailor in a small Sunfish.

So many years ago, she and her mother had loved sailing this particular stretch of the Colorado River. Almost every Saturday until she was fourteen, they would rent a boat, pack a picnic lunch, and spend the day together sailing, laughing, talking. Just the two of them.

That was the last time in her life that she could remember feeling totally safe.

A knock on the suite door startled her, but she remained where she was, letting Janko deal with it. He was right about working out an OP. Without a strong one, they would be as adrift as that small boat without a rudder.

"KC, lunch."

She walked back in, leaving the doors open, but stopped in mid-stride when she saw the table. He'd arranged the covered plates across from each other, the utensils were half hidden inside the folds of cloth napkins, and a single yellow rose had replaced the carnation.

The condemned's last meal?
No way in hell.

She straightened, took a deep breath, and was renewed by a surge of confidence, determination and energy. Time to get down, get dirty, get her children back, then get the hell out. No longer did she think of herself as Kelly, the ex-wife and mother. Beyond a shadow of a doubt, she was once more KC, the cold efficient killer he'd trained her to be.

He motioned for her to sit as she walked the few steps that separated them, then he pulled out her chair, seating her.

She cautiously eyed him as she lifted the stainless steel lid, not sure what to expect. The aroma of spicy grilled chicken wafted up and she closed her eyes. It was all she could do not to lick her lips as her mouth watered.

"I...I'm sorry if it's not what you wanted. We could trade." He sounded as if he was trying to please her. As if she mattered to him. *Ha! Not likely in this lifetime.*

Opening her eyes, she inspected her sandwich first before stealing a glance at his. Her onion roll looked more delicious than his plain hamburger bun, and she couldn't fail to notice that he'd asked for a side of ranch dressing instead of mayonnaise. A tiny bottle of ketchup squatted next to the miniature salt and pepper shakers.

How like him to remember her choices of condiments, chicken versus beef. And he'd brought her favorite colored rose, just like old times. So different from Randy, who'd lived with her for years and couldn't have guessed even one of her preferences if his life had depended on it. Which fortunately for him, it never had.

But after all this time, Janko hadn't forgotten. A lump formed in her throat, threatening to choke her. Those little things that he'd done for her everyday was the way he'd shown his love. Her heart drummed a bit harder as she recalled the first time they'd had lunch at a hotel. He'd surprised her with a yellow rose, then taken it back to slowly run it down her nose, past her lips trailing it in between her breasts. Their lunch had grown cold as she silently urged him to explore her body.

Warmth spread through her now and she cleared her throat as she mentally cleared her thoughts. But she couldn't help smiling at him.

"Thanks, but this is just fine." The funny thing was she meant it. After spreading the ranch dressing on one side of the roll, she added stone-ground mustard from another little jar to the other side, then rebuilt her sandwich of melted pepper-jack cheese, chicken, lettuce, tomato and red onion. A big thick slice of red onion. She wasn't planning on killing anyone with her breath, or kissing anyone either, especially him. Just before attacking her creation, she caught him smiling at her as if could read her mind. "What's so funny?"

"Nothing. Merely enjoying the scenery."

"Sheesh. Give me a break, would ya?" she sighed as she rolled her eyes heavenward. Her half-hearted protest couldn't stop the inward grin at his sophomoric flirtation. "What does Delacourt look like now?"

"Older. Fatter. Slower," he said between bites of his burger.

She picked up her pickle spear and pointed it at him. "You know, as I remember Del, he wasn't the sharpest tool in the shed."

"Still isn't." He leaned across the table and took a bite of the dill. "You shouldn't point. It's not polite."

Refusing to yield to the temptation of responding with a crude remark, she finished off the pickle. "Why Austin? Why so far away from Pegasus?"

"It's not so far from Tulsa, or Oklahoma City."

"But it's not close, either. In fact, it's one of the last places—"

"That anyone would think of."

"And one of the most illogical. I grew up here." She was going to add that she knew the city like the back of her hand, yet only today, she hadn't been sure where they'd landed. Putting down her sandwich, she absently trailed a french fry through the pool of ketchup on her plate. She had been gone a long time—a whole lifetime.

"So..." She paused, debating whether to eat the cold fry. "Where do we begin?"

"Good question. The only solid clue I have is a hotel confirmation number and this weekend's date, but I don't know the hotel." Finishing the last bite of his burger, he wiped his hands on the napkin, then drew a slip of paper from his pocket.

"Let me see." She took it from him, then studied it for a moment. Gun Show 634H1412 AUS3345 The numbers didn't look familiar to her. "Where did you get this?"

He pushed his plate away before getting up. "From a note pad on Delacourt's desk."

"He left a copy?"

"Of course not. In his office, I noticed a note pad lying

on a stack of gun show flyers from all over the country."

Moving her plate to the center of the table, she examined the paper again. "Del was into gun shows? He didn't seem to be the collector type."

"He'd been going for some time now and was always trying to get Pegasus to spring for the trips. Related business, he claimed." Janko finished the rest of her fries.

"That sounds like Delacourt, but what made you suspect anything?"

"His desk looked messier than normal, not that he was neat and organized to begin with, but like he'd left in a hurry. I took the pad back to my office, and on a hunch, rubbed the surface with pencil lead. This is what came up."

"Do you have the original?"

"Sure."

While Janko was rifling through his briefcase, she got up to place the other half of her sandwich in the mini-fridge, and spied a white Styrofoam container. "What's this?"

"Huh?" He looked across the room to the container she held up, then to her. "Oh, that. Chocolate marble cheesecake. Just in case I struck out with lunch, you'd still have something to eat." He flashed her a half-cocked smile that once made her insides melt.

Who could resist cheesecake, or the bearer of such delicious enticements? She shrugged her shoulders in dismay. He was trying to cover all the bases. And there had been a time that he'd covered certain parts of her with cheesecake, then taken his own sweet time making sure she got clean. She slammed the door to the fridge and to her thoughts, then joined him by the couch.

He handed her the sheet of paper, now covered with pencil. "How did you know that AUS was Austin and not Australia or Austria? We've been to all those places."

His clipped laugh drew her gaze to his and held her spellbound. A jolt she'd never known before passed through her. She gasped, breaking the connection. My

God, what had just happened? Had he experienced it too? *Get a grip, girl.*

"Hey." Janko snapped his fingers. "Earth to KC. Are you zoned?"

"No, no. I'm fine. Go on." But was she? He hadn't seemed to be affected at all, which was lucky for her.

"Like I was saying, Delacourt was a strictly white world operator. He wasn't cleared for overseas duty, besides his passport was still in his desk."

She focused on the second set of letters and numbers first. Why did they look so familiar? 3345. Of course, it's March, the first 3, and 3, 4, 5 are Friday, Saturday, and Sunday. The first set seemed longer than a simple hotel confirmation. Did it reference a flight number? A house number? She just didn't have a clue. Turning the paper over, she held it up to the light. "This looks like an 'I' to me, not a one, then the letters could mean either the Hilton or Holiday Inn."

Going to the coffee table, she opened the drawer and took out the phone book. Looking under the H's, she ran her finger down the listings until she found the Hilton reservation number.

In a perfect imitation of a nasal-twanged receptionist, she spoke, "Con-foirm-ming con-foir-ma-tion num-ba six-tree-four—." She winked broadly at him. "Oh, we-ll, you don't say. Ciao." Hanging up the phone, she went back to the directory and started over again, having to repeat the number twice.

"Yes, could I have the phys-sical address for your ho-tel for Mr. and Mrs. William B. Smith?" She gave him a thumb's up sign. "Mr. Smith's already checked in? Thank you so ve-ery much. Ciao." She hung up the phone, then sat on the edge of the couch, anticipation dancing through like an electric current.

"Holiday Inn on I-35 and Town Lake. He's so damn close—just across the river. We *are* going to pay him a little visit?"

"You bet. We'll surprise him at his own game." He

sounded as excited as she was.

During the short drive, she went down a mental checklist of possible situations, moves, and counter plays. She glanced over at Janko's stony face. He was probably running through the ops plan, too. They fit so well as a team that his silence didn't bother her. Endless planning and stupid chatter, that's what set her teeth on edge.

He pulled the car into the crowded hotel parking lot and she looked out at Town Lake, with barely a ripple across the surface. Calm and at ease on top, but one helluva current flowed underneath, exactly like her.

"Hold it." He stopped her as she opened the car door.

Looking over, she saw he held a small gun. "Honey," she whispered.

"A present from Murphy."

Her fingers brushed his palm as she took the gun. It was still warm from his grasp.

"Just in case. But, KC—" he eyed her soberly. "We need Del alive."

She nodded, then climbed out of the car. While he opened the trunk to remove a small flight bag, she took a moment to untuck her T-shirt and put the gun inside the front waistband of her jeans. She tried to smooth some of the wrinkles from the cotton material and made sure that nothing showed before following him into the hotel.

Detouring around a pile of luggage, she walked through the double set of glass doors. Chaos abounded in the lobby as people congregated in small groups with the check-in line winding past the elevators several feet away.

She tugged him aside as a group of teenage girls charged past them, headed for the pool. "This place is a madhouse." Her gaze never stopped scanning the crowd.

"Notice anything unusual?"

"Yeah, VFM." She winked at him. "Very few men."

"That should make Delacourt easier to spot."

Then, as if a light bulb turned on, she knew how to get into his room without tipping him off. "I'll be right back," she said, then made her way to the front desk.

Waiting until the clerk was swamped, KC slapped her hand on the counter. "Hey, you didn't give me a key to my room."

"Which room?" The harassed woman never glanced up.

"Oh, hell, I don't remember. Y'all never put the room numbers on those paper thingies. William Smith. William B. Smith—Mr. and Mrs." Picking up a pen, she tapped it impatiently on the granite surface. "Marie? Is that your name? I'm waiting."

Marie passed a credit card receipt to another guest, then said frostily, "If you'll step to the side, I'll help you in a moment."

"Fine. I'll discuss my treatment and your attitude with your manager." KC stepped back, ready to leave when the woman spoke.

"Wait, Mrs. Smith." She looked at the computer screen as she rapidly typed on the keyboard. "I'll need to see some form of identification before I can issue you another set of key cards."

"Oh for Pete's sake! Does it take an act of God to get a key? Well, I've never—" she turned to a teenage girl next to her— "you're going to be old enough to vote before you get checked in here."

Marie glared at KC through narrowed eyes. "I'm sorry, but there are rules I have to follow."

"Hey, just give the lady what she wants. My team has gotta check in then get to the ball game." The sound of Janko's deep voice from behind KC made her smile.

"Be quick about it. You've got a whole lobby full of people waiting to get into their rooms."

Harrumphing loudly, the clerk keyed two plastic cards, slipped it into a folder and boldly wrote 225 on the inside before passing it across the counter. "I'm sorry, Mrs. Smith, for the inconvenience. You'll have to give Mr. Smith this new one."

"Thank you," KC replied haughtily as she scooped up the folder, then disappeared into the crowd. Janko met her at the elevators and they rode up together. Room 225 was at the end of the dimly lit hall that seemed to stretch forever.

At the door, they could hear a TV blaring. KC paused to look at him. He tilted his head to the right and she to the left before putting the key in. The click of the lock and door handle sounded as loud as gunshots as he flung the door open.

"Honey, I'm ho-ome," she cried hoping the element of surprise would catch Delacourt off guard. Rolling to the left, she came up in a crouch with her gun drawn and ready as Janko took several steps into the room.

"Clear," he said, then immediately followed with, "Ah, hell."

She straightened to see what had caused him to curse. Sitting on the couch was a very naked Delacourt.

A very dead Delacourt.

"Ga-wd, he's uglier than I remembered." Her stomach roiled as she saw the sightless bulging eyes in the contorted blue face. A line of drool hung from the corner of his mouth to the fat, food-covered chest. One arm lay by his side and the other rested on his rotund hairy belly. She averted her gaze to the overturned Chinese take-out cartons strewn on the carpet. "What a pig."

She decocked her gun, slipped it into the back waistband of her jeans, then stepped closer as Janko inspected the body.

"He hasn't been dead long. No rigor." He checked Del's head. "I don't smell anything that would lead me to think he was poisoned."

"Ack, how can you tell with all that crap on him?" It took a tremendous amount of willpower not to kick the dead man. Her attention snapped back to Janko when he picked up a chopstick and pried open the dead man's mouth. "Well?"

"Ah, Del, gluttony has become your undoing." He dropped the chopstick on the couch, then flashed her a tight smile. "What a way to go."

Slipping back into pro-mode, she critically eyed the body. "We've done worse. So, you think he choked to death rather than a heart attack? Like I really care." She folded her arms across her chest, then tipped her head to one side. "Wish we could have questioned him. He'd still be dead, but I would have really enjoyed making his last few moments pure terror."

"Darlin', you're quite good at terrorizing a man. There's no doubt, you could have found out who held Del's leash. Too bad our lead's as dead as he is." He moved away from the couch, but stopped. "I'll take the bed and bathroom while you cover this one."

"Fine."

"Oh, geez, I hate it when you women say, 'fine' like that." She couldn't suppress a chuckle. "Fine," she added for good measure.

Muffled sounds of cheering broke into her consciousness, making her glance at the television as teenage girls ran on a basketball court.

The commentator interjected, "At the beginning of the season, no one could have predicted the schools represented here at the Erwin Center. Whether they're 5A or 1A, the big guns come out as teams just seem to rise to a higher quality when playing for the state championship. Tonight's games will decide which teams make it into the finals."

"Janko, come here." She waited until he stood beside her, then pointed at the TV. "That's where Delacourt was going to take us. I just know it. It's perfect. Lots of teenage girls, adoring mothers, fathers and grandparents. Never underestimate the power of basketball. Fans will be pouring in to watch every championship game, regardless of who's playing. I can promise you that more than a few fights will break out, so any commotion we would have made could easily have been overlooked or ignored."

"Hide in plain sight." Janko combed his fingers through his hair. "That's so typical it has agency stamped all over it. See if you can find something that might tip us to who or where he was supposed to meet." He walked to the open closet and began rifling through a suitcase, then disappeared to search the bathroom.

"There's nothing here but trash," she muttered while picking around in a messy briefcase overfilled with scraps of paper. Slamming the case closed, she glanced around the room once. Then again. On the far lamp table, a spot of bright orange underneath a carton of food snagged her attention.

She crossed the room and stood looking at what she'd already suspected would be there. Knocking the carton to the floor, she peeled three tickets to the State Finals on Saturday afternoon from the pool of congealing grease.

But actually holding the evidence and the reality of what could have been—might have been—made her stomach do a couple of flip-flops before settling like a ton of lead. She'd been on target, and so had Janko.

She stopped in front of Delacourt. The man she'd called a friend. The man who'd been sent to kidnap her and her daughter. The man who'd been sent to kill her son. She couldn't remain detached as heat flooded her body and hate consumed her. A shudder of revulsion snaked up her spine as she thought about those grub-white hands with the dirt-encrusted nails and stubby fingers touching her or her children. If Janko hadn't intervened...

And she snapped.

"You fat, mother-fuckin' bastard!" Pulling the gun from her waistband, she centered it on his forehead.

Chapter Six

As Janko eased his fingers down KC's arm, her tension vibrated through him like an electric charge, causing the hair on the back of his neck to stand up. Even though her face was composed, he knew she was ready for vengeance. "Save it until it can do some good. Let's get out of here before Del starts stinking up the place."

She narrowed her eyes. "Too late."

If she found it necessary to shoot Delacourt to release her bottled rage, that was fine by him. The risk of detection from her .22 would be minimum. The noise wouldn't even be heard above the TV. And if someone were in the next room, they would probably mistake the shot as a shoot out on some crime show, or the slamming of a cabinet door.

He let his hand drop to his side as he waited for her to pull the trigger. *Talk about spicing up a routine investigation when the cops found a dead man with a gunshot to the forehead that wasn't the cause of death. Oh well, it wasn't anything he couldn't cover up.*

Blinking a couple of times, she relaxed her shoulders, then lowered her gun. He exhaled a small pent up breath as she stuffed the pistol into her waistband.

"If you're ready, you go first, and be careful." He stepped in front of her, blocking her way as he made sure her emotions were in check. "We're not in the clear yet."

She stared at him, then walked out. He gave the room a quick visual before slipping away. Taking a different route through the hotel, he crossed the parking lot from the opposite direction and met her at the car. He used the remote to unlock the car, climbing in at the same time she did.

"We have a date for the Saturday afternoon game." She waved tickets in front of his nose, half blinding him as he left the lot.

"Really? Been a long time, hasn't it." He waited for her to slam him with a retort, but her silence caused him to give her a sidelong glance. She was running both hands up and down her jeans. She opened her mouth, but didn't speak.

"What's wrong?"

"I feel... dirty... contaminated. I don't have anything to change into."

Was that all? He wanted to laugh, to tell her it was just a woman thing, but she appeared more vulnerable, and damn it, more beautiful than ever before.

So he merely nodded and maneuvered the car through traffic, then stopped at a campus clothing store. She gathered her hair into both hands, lifted it off her shoulders, exposing her long graceful neck. And he knew exactly where to kiss that gorgeous nape to turn her to liquid in his arms.

Damn, he had no business thinking about getting in her pants. Was it because she was in danger, and the thrill of the hunt turned him on?

"You coming or staying?" She was leaning through the open car door, a scowl on her face.

Oh yeah, babe, I wish I was coming. "I'm right behind you."

He followed her in, standing close as she methodically looked through the rack of shirts, examining each one in turn—no matter how similar they were. For God's sake, a shirt is a shirt, he wanted to tell her. Naively, he'd assumed she would go in, pick up a few things, and they'd be on their way.

Hell, he hated wasting time on something so inconsequential. Raking his fingers through his hair, he tempered his normal impatience. He should be grateful they had a few peaceful moments together. One minute she'd have that soft-eyed look when she spoke about her kids, then the next, she could turn on him like a lioness protecting her cubs. He couldn't predict, or control, when her claws would dig into him. Why was she so angry with him? After all, he'd saved her and her children's lives. But instead of thanking him, she seemed to hate him. Of course, she certainly had good reason, given his track record with her.

Would he ever understand her?

A flash through the window sent an alarm through him as he keyed on eliminating a possible source of danger. After assessing that the light had come from a passing car, his gaze scanned the sparsely populated store, stopping when he caught their reflection in the three-way mirror.

This past week had been hard on them both, but she'd taken the worst news that possibly a parent could deal with. It showed in the dark circles under her eyes, the hollowness in her cheekbones, the weight loss that caused her clothes to sag. But now that he was close to her again, he realized she still had the power to make him weak with need, to make him want to bury himself deep inside her. His body temperature rose a few hundred degrees thinking about it.

He followed her to a display of shorts, where the selection process started over. She loaded her arm with several styles, then left him cooling his heels outside the dressing room door. After what seemed an eternity, he walked outside for some fresh air. He understood why his father had always warned him to never go shopping with his mother and sister. Were *all* women this obsessive? Taking a couple deep breaths to bolster his resolve, he wandered back into the store and found her in front of a wall of athletic shoes.

"Now what are you doing?" His exasperation leaked out with each word.

She wheeled to face him with her fisted hands on her hips and whispered harshly, "Do you expect me to wear my Ropers or combat boots with shorts? Thought I was expected to blend in, or would you prefer I just hang a sign around my neck with my name on it?" She gave him a long steely look, then selected a pair of white leather running shoes.

"Right. Take all the time you need." He handed her a wad of bills, eager to escape before she chewed him up again. So much for civility.

She finally came out carrying a large orange and white bag. At the car, he opened her door first, grinning when she shot him a one-eyebrow-raised glare before getting in. "My mama taught me to open a lady's door." Her gruff sheesh wasn't lost on him as he walked around to his side. "Where would you like to go now?"

"I'd like to get out of these jeans and into a hot tub for a long overdue soak." An exhausted sigh punctuated the last word.

And I'd like to help you out of those jeans, he thought as he exited the lot.

Afternoon classes from the university had dismissed, which sent a stream of students across the street, forcing traffic to slow. He watched kids and cars weave around each other, and something niggling in the back of his mind clicked.

"Have you had any contact with agency personnel since you left?" He could feel waves of hostility emanating from her as she stared straight ahead.

"No. Why?"

"Who knows you have kids?" Based on her *I'm never going to* attitude when they were together, he never considered that she would change her mind. Or that someone would change it for her.

"Everyone in Treaty Hill. Pregnancy is a hard condition to hide for very long, especially in a small town."

In his imagination he pictured her walking around Seven Oaks in the early morning sunshine, her belly swollen enough to cast its own shadow. He saw her, beautiful and regal, commanding him and a bevy of servants to obey her slightest whim. And for a moment, his chest tightened, making it hard to breathe, as he became jealous that her ex-husband had shared that special time.

Where did that thought come from? I don't even like kids.

He shuddered inwardly and forced his mind back to finding some sense of this whole mess. "Why kids and why you?" he muttered.

She skewered him with her gaze. "What's it to you if I chose to have children? You'll never know the joy, the pride, the love you get from having a child in your life. There's more in this world than just thinking about yourself."

He drove on a few more blocks as her words sank in. She was right to an extent, but also wrong. "Kids are inherently selfish, and they can bring as much heartache as happiness." The heartaches he'd suffered had been enough to fill two lifetimes, and there wasn't enough happiness in the world worth that risk.

"Your point?" Her lips compressed into a tight line as she radiated righteous indignation.

"Some people are meant to be parents."

"And some aren't," she spit back at him.

"We're getting off the subject. What I meant was why Delacourt was sent after you and Ashley, and not Tyler. Your daughter is the pivotal point."

"Ashley? No way. She can't be." KC faced him, refusing to believe what he had said, refusing to delve into the possibility that he was right.

"Think back over the last week, did you notice anything peculiar or unusual that might have happened?" His face showed his concentration as he freed them from the congested campus traffic, then drove on toward the hotel. "Nothing out of the ordinary? No hang up phone calls? No strangers showing up?"

Her hands flew up as she went on the defensive. "I know what you're getting at, that I couldn't protect my family because I was lax. Wrong. I live on a ranch. There are strangers coming in all the time to talk about horses. I buy, sell, and train horses, and sometimes people stop because they're plain lost. So don't preach that I'm not cognizant of my surroundings.

"As for phone calls, get real! I have a teenager and when she isn't on the phone, Tyler's on the Internet. If we did have any suspicious calls, I'd be the last to know about it. And you're wrong about Ashley. She simply can't be the key player in this nightmare."

Now in underground parking, neither the temperature inside nor outside the car cooled with the shade. It took her eyes a few minutes to adjust as Janko pulled into a space. She snapped up her bags from the back seat, then was off at a fast clip to the elevators before he shifted the car into park. Mashing the call button over and over, she knew it wouldn't make it arrive any faster than if she'd just pushed it once. It made her feel better though, and that counted for something.

"KC. Wait." She heard him call as the doors opened.

Not a chance. Scooting inside, she thought she'd made her escape as the doors slid shut but he managed to wedge first his foot then squeeze his body through the narrow opening before the metal panels sprang wide.

The air inside the elevator was rancid, the space becoming claustrophobic, forcing her to take shallow breaths. Janko was right, she had noticed a white sedan that appeared almost everywhere she went. But she'd blown it off because of the Spring Festival traffic, and that make and model of car was a popular rental. Had she been under surveillance? She knew positively that it hadn't been Delacourt. She would have recognized him. Maybe it had been an investigative reporter since she'd refused all interviews after the tractor explosion at the fair.

Lost in thought, she absently followed Janko when he

exited on their floor, then into their room. Whoever was after them, Ashley was not the target, of that she was sure. Totally drained, she dropped her clothes bags to the floor.

"I'll give you a few minutes to settle in." He opened the door again, then paused in the hallway. "Don't leave."

Irritation revived her flagging energy. Like he could tell her what she could and couldn't do? Leaving the room hadn't even entered her mind until he mentioned it. She retrieved her bags as she went into the bedroom, took out a change of clothes before stuffing the rest in her duffle. As she stepped into the bathroom, the idea of a long soothing soak complete with all the goodies made her change course for the hotel gift shop.

She deserved a little pampering, and if she could relax, maybe she'd be able to piece things together. She plucked the key card from the table, then poking her head out the door, checked to see if the coast was clear before sneaking down the stairs.

Smug and feeling a bit self-righteous as she entered the gift shop, she made her selections of toiletries, then stopped at the small boutique next to the gift shop. She charged her purchase of a satin nightgown to the room. With a quick surveillance of the lobby, she scurried back to the elevator with her loot.

****

Janko had moved the car to the first level of the parking garage, noting the means of exits, then headed back for the hotel. After KC was safe inside the room, he'd taken a walk to give her time to shower and change, and himself a chance to assess the surroundings. While this place wasn't much different than the hundreds he'd been in before, he wanted to be familiar with the layout. Low shrubs and plenty of lighting circled the perimeter of the hotel. The outside doors were strictly key access, but not a true safety measure. Anyone who wanted in could either walk through the lobby, or wait for an employee or guest to enter and slip in. Still, the doors probably deterred some of the large crowd that camped on the hotel's riverbank property to watch the bats leave.

He entered the hotel and ducked into the first stairwell. The flat beige walls absorbed most of the light from a low wattage bulb making the space as dark and narrow as his thoughts. *If I had protected her better, she wouldn't be in danger.* He slammed his fist against the metal door. The thudding echo mocked him. *If you love her, she'll die. She'll die, and so will I. I won't love her.* He still had no clue who was after her, but he'd find them. After all, he was the best at hunting people. It wasn't the first time he'd faced a nameless enemy—that had been business—this was personal. She was involved. He'd tried to put her out of harm's way fifteen years ago, to give her a normal life, a safe life, without the agency, without him. Despite his efforts, here she was, in danger again. He'd failed to protect her.

A sliver of fear speared him in the chest as he thought of her alone in room. What if they'd been followed? Nah, he'd have sensed it, he always had. But what if... He took the stairs two at a time, ignoring the burning sensation in his legs as he passed floor after floor. At the seventh landing he stopped to catch his breath, silently berating himself for not exercising more and smoking less. As his breathing and heart rate slowed, he opened the door a crack to check the hallway, then calmly walked to the room.

Silence and emptiness greeted him as he entered the suite. A lamp illuminated part of the living room, and the curtains had been drawn, but everything else was the same as when he'd left. He growled as he swung both glass doors into the dark bedroom. Maybe she'd gone down to the restaurant or the gift shop for more shopping after he'd told her not to leave. Then a thin beam of light from under the bathroom door caught his attention.

"KC?" he whispered as he eased the door open, finding her asleep in the tub. Her left hand, draped over the tub rim, had gone slack and a piece of paper had drifted to the floor next to a half-empty drink. Beige colored candles, with their vanilla scent, filled the room with a soft glow that turned her skin golden.

A twinge of guilt tapped him. He really should wake her. Better yet, the proper thing would be to leave, but he'd never been proper where she was concerned. And he wasn't going to start now.

She looked more alluring than he remembered. Several tendrils of blond hair had escaped the pile on top of her head, framing her face. Her sensual lips had given him more pleasure than a man deserved. The slow rise and fall of her chest made the water lap gently against her breasts. Taking a step closer, he wanted to cup them and let his tongue traced patterns on her dusky-rose nipples.

Blood pounded in his ears as his gaze continued to her slightly rounded belly, and ground to a halt at the triangle of light brown curls. He flexed his fingers to quell the temptation to see if they were still silky. Images of them indulging in rip-your-clothes-off, can't-wait-another minute sex left his knees weak, forcing him to lean against the counter for support and to ease the pain of his growing erection.

Oh, Lord, he hurt. A raw aching need spread through him like a wildfire. His desire trapped him, leaving him only moments away from spontaneous combustion. As a frustrated groan escaped him, she opened one eye.

"Don't I get *any* privacy?" She didn't bother to cover herself, but instead reached for her drink.

Moving quickly, he picked up the glass, grateful for the closer view, and miserable knowing that he would have no relief tonight. He poured the rest of a tiny bottle of Scotch into her glass, then set it near her hand. "How's your bath?"

She took a sip, and put the glass down before giving him a momentary gaze that seared his body. "Better without company. I'll be out in a moment."

As much as he didn't want to, he left the bathroom

and walked to the mini-fridge, grabbed a bottle of water, then wrenched off the cap. Taking a long drink did nothing to cool him as he imagined her climbing from the tub. What was she drying at that precise moment? The room grew hotter and smaller, driving him onto the balcony. As the cool humid breeze from the river washed over him, he could have sworn he heard his skin sizzling.

When she came to stand behind him, her body heat transferred to him. He turned and her gaze, smoky and unwavering, held his for a drawn out second. Then she slowly undid the belt of her white terry robe, allowing it to fall open. He pulled one side back until he could see her breast. His body responded, growing harder as she revealed her other breast. Her nipples puckered and tightened under his hot stare. She stepped closer, and he drew in an intoxicating breath filled with her fresh floral scent instead of the faint musty river air.

Moistening her lips, she kissed his cheek, then his jaw. He shuddered. Her touch was enough to make him come. Unable to resist any longer, he cupped her face, pulling her to him. His mouth tenderly joined with hers and her lips were as soft and sweet as he'd remembered. When she deepened their kiss, he hungrily claimed her, demanding more.

She stiffened. Her hand braced against his chest, scorched his skin, making it difficult to breathe.

"I'm sorry," she whispered.

Disappointment gripped him as he watched her go to the bedroom. The door eased shut. He grudgingly admitted that it was too fast, too soon, and too damn bad. Pivoting on his heel, he grasped the balcony railing, the cool iron cutting into his hands, but the pain wouldn't relieve his frustration. Just being near her wasn't enough, he wanted her like he never had before. He wasn't a patient man, but this time he'd wait. Wait for her to come to him.

Taking a few uneven breaths, he concentrated on the reflection of the full moon on the water. The rippling surface distorted, but couldn't change, the image. Maybe that was what KC thought of him, that his outward appearance was altered by age, but inside he was the same cold bastard. Removing his shirt, he tossed it behind him before lighting a cigarette, then tucked the pack in his jeans. He debated going inside, although he doubted he'd get any sleep on the couch, not with KC filling his mind.

She was definitely more emotional than when she was younger, but maybe that had to do with her children. He admired her complete devotion to them, was amazed by her ability to focus all her energy, and most of all was in awe of her unconditional love. Sadly, that was something that wasn't in him.

Flicking his cigarette into the air, he watched the glowing butt until it landed in the grass below, where it winked a few times, then went out. For years, he'd treated his memory of her like that. Taking it out, enjoying it for a few minutes, then stamping it out. But he'd been deceiving himself because she was a part of him that he could never give up.

And could never have.

The moon had crossed to the west, and the night sounds had switched from rowdy pedestrians and vehicular traffic to a lonely owl screeching, and the frogs along the riverbank were croaking sad songs.

He'd started reaching for another cigarette when her terrified screams sent him running inside. His heart raced as he flung wide the double doors. The outside security light washed the bedroom in an orange fluorescence that made her movements appear jerky and uncoordinated as she crawled across the bed, searching the covers as she screamed her children's names.

"Wake up! KC, wake up." Grabbing her arms, he brought her to him, her unblinking eyes glazed as her nightmare continued. He shook her lightly, but she broke his hold.

"Let me goooo. My kids are gone... help me. Help me

find them." She took a few steps away, then returned to sit on the bed and clutched a pillow to her chest. "My children."

Watching as she rocked back and forth, he saw her face wet with tears, and it tore at his heart. He desperately wanted to wrap his arms around her to make her pain disappear, but he was afraid. Afraid she would push him away. Afraid he would lose the tenuous grip he had on his emotions.

Afraid he would love her again.

But when her body began quaking, he forgot his fears, forgot about the consequences as he sat on the bed beside her. Tugging the pillow away, he crooned, "Ashley and Tyler are fine. They're safe, babe. I've made sure of that."

She surprised him by burying her face in his chest. "My children...they're all right?" Her muffled words were hot puffs on his skin.

"No one can hurt them." He gathered her to him and rested his back against the headboard. She fit so good, so right in his arms. Laying his head on hers, he kissed the top of it, then stroked her hair until her body relaxed.

From within the warmth of his arms, KC pulled herself together. *What am I doing turning to Janko for comfort?* Because it'd been a damn long time since anyone had bothered to offer her any solace. Because she wanted to trust him again. Because she needed to believe in him again.

"Thanks," she said, her voice wavering but not cracking. She made no effort to move away from him, instead snuggling closer when he tucked the covers around them. The sound of his heart beating and his even breathing dissolved the last vestiges of her nightmare. At last she'd found a semblance of peace that allowed her to forget all the bad things that had happened since they'd been apart. A peace she wanted to get lost in.

When his arm loosened from her shoulder, she thought he'd fallen asleep. Turning her head, she saw that he was watching her. A faint smile parted his lips, causing her body to awaken with a desire she'd believed had died long ago.

Reaching up, she traced the outline of his jaw, then kissed him, tentatively at first. And when he responded, a tortured whimper escaped from her throat as a fire ignited within her. Gone was all reservation, all hesitation, and all her false pride. Wanting, no, the desperate *need* to have him, consumed her. She pulled him closer, but it wasn't enough. Her hands skimmed across his broad shoulders, then circled his chest. The feel of the crisp hair there sent jagged currents of sensation through her, making her ache for skin to skin contact. Fumbling with the button on his jeans, she couldn't free what her hand desired to touch.

He slid her gown up until he cupped her breast, his thumb and forefinger gently rolling her nipple between them. It was sweet torture, a pleasure she didn't want to end even as he helped her shed the flimsy satin encumbrance. Easing onto her back, she lay naked, exposed, vulnerable before him.

He stood, slowly undid the rest of the buttons on his jeans, then skinned out of the denim, freeing his erection. *Oh Lord.* She reached to touch him, but he stopped her, placing her arm above her head, causing her breast to rise. Very gently, he lowered his mouth over her throbbing nipple, sucking deeply, exerting a force that connected to her core. She moaned softly as his hand floated along her ribs, her belly, then began to rub light circles on her mound.

Wanting him to go lower, she parted her legs to expose her throbbing need, but he didn't touch her. She thought she'd go crazy as he stroked everywhere but there. When he straddled her, she prepared to accept him, only to have him suckle her other breast, then leave a trail of hot kisses down her body. His hands stroked her inner thighs as he lowered his head. The stubble along his jaw line rasped against her tender skin, heightening the sensation of her pulsing nub. He nuzzled the juncture where her legs joined her body, then his hot breath fanned her pubic hair. Her fingers plowed through his hair as her aching increased.

When his lips parted her, she drew in a long ragged gasp. His tongue made feathery explorations until he found her sensitive tip of flesh, then began alternately flicking and sucking on it. She arched her body against his mouth, holding onto his shoulders, scared of the sensations swirling through her, more scared that he would stop.

His tender ministrations dissolved her fears away and sent her into an upward spiral of nerve-tingling, cell-screaming awareness striving to reach that pinnacle. And when she was on the edge of shattering, he slid inside, filling her with his heated length. Meeting his thrust with a force of her own, she climbed higher until she came, her world splintering into jagged shards of pulses and prickles. Wrapping her quivering legs around his hips, she clenched against him as they moved as one.

Hearing his strangled cry as he came, she couldn't help but smile—for the pleasure given and taken. Her bones were rubbery, her body still slick and hot and oh-so-sated. The air caressing them smelled of sex.

He started to speak, but she put her finger across his mouth. "Don't ruin the mood." When he rolled to his back, she settled into the hollow of his shoulder, her fingers tracing patterns on his chest. It had been too long since she'd felt attractive, sensual, loved. Too long since she'd been with Janko. She had no regrets.

And she damn sure wasn't ready for it to be over.

Chapter Seven

The numbers on the clock beside the bed hadn't changed since the last time he'd looked. He checked his watch and the second hand jumped once for every two of his heartbeats.

Almost time.

As nervous as a caged animal, he paced around the small hotel room, then stopped at the mirror to critically eye his appearance. The love handles were gone, but he was just not dedicated enough to work for washboard abs. Would she notice?

Would she care?

His face now had more character than he'd been born with. Paying top dollar, he knew every nip, tuck and fine surgical line was well hidden and all the pain had been worth it. A small smirk caused his full lips to thin slightly as they curved upward. Even in the prime of his life, he had never looked better than this.

Good things come to those who wait. And he'd been good, oh so good. He'd waited for this day, planned for this day, and been as patient as Job. But now the man grew restless. He hadn't heard from Delacourt since yesterday afternoon.

Why hadn't he called this morning? Fat stinking slob. Never could follow any plan right.

"Jesus, Mary and Joseph," he swore softly. He hated working with morons. His whole life he'd dealt with stupid people. They were everywhere, and too obtuse to know they were idiots. Fortunately for him, after their usefulness was gone, so were they.

Loose lips sink ships. He left no loose ends that could trip him up because he was too smart for that. Withdrawing the gun from the leather shoulder holster he wore, he pulled back the slide, then smiled when he heard the metallic sound as the bullet chambered. His body throbbed as it always did when he thought about death. He returned the pistol to the holster as he glanced around the room. There were things he had to do before he could leave.

Removing his bag from the closet shelf, he took it into the bathroom to pack the few personal items he'd used last night. Once that was done, he got a clean towel from the rack, placed it on the counter, then turned on the hot water. As he waited for the water to steam, he dumped the coffee grounds into the plastic trashcan liner, closed it, picked up both the trash and his bag, then placed them on a chair by the door. The bathroom mirror had clouded over and revealed no traces of his presence. He washed and dried the coffeepot, his only glass and cup. Using the same damp towel, he methodically wiped down the bathroom, then the bedroom, removing as much incidental matter as he could. He stripped the linens from the bed. There was nothing he could do about loose hair on the carpet, but he didn't have much left anyway. Wadding the sheets together, he threw them next to his bag, then checked his watch again.

Almost time.

Only ten minutes had passed. Sighing wearily, he thought about verifying the hour with the television, but that'd be something else he'd have to clean. He gave the easy chair cushion a shake to remove any traces that he'd sat there last night. Slipping into a lightweight jacket, he zipped it halfway so his gun was concealed, then stuck a baseball cap on his head.

With everything gathered up, he wiped both knobs, headed for the next floor up using the stairs, then left his trash in a big container next to the ice machine. Finding a maid's cart already down the hall, he buried the linens from his room under the dirty stack.

His obsession about not leaving a trail was an asset not a liability. More than once, he'd left crimes scenes with no traceable evidence.

After paying his hotel bill, the man walked to the parking lot. The sun tinged the spring sky with pink and purple streaks. He threw his arms wide and breathed deeply. *It's a beautiful day. A perfect day. A day made just for me. Nothing but the best for me.*

He calmly strolled to his white panel van, opened the side door and tossed his bag inside. Sliding in, he picked up a pillow, held it to his chest, then nuzzled it.

Almost time.

He imagined her lying on it, thanking him for his thoughtfulness, his caring. Giving it a couple of fluffs, he laid it between the two sets of handcuffs he'd bolted to the floorboard. His hands brushed the nap of the carpet, making it look darker.

The new car aroma excited him. He hoped she'd be as excited to see him. If not, he patted the small green bag he'd filled with sedatives, in time she would.

He glanced at his watch.

Showtime.

Now was the time to reclaim what had been stolen from him.

Now was the time to get his daughter back.

****

The crowds at the Erwin Center were just as loud as KC had expected. A gang of kids hurrying down the aisle bumped her into the lap of very surprised man. Excusing herself, she continued to the designated seats, only to find two of the three occupied. She rechecked her tickets.

"Move, lady. Me 'n Rick can't see the game."

"Excuse me, isn't this row 5, seats a, b?"

"Yeah, what of it?" His continuous black eyebrow undulated like a furry caterpillar.

"I think you have the wrong seats."

"Too bad. We got here first, so what are you going to do about it?" He elbowed his buddy, who nodded at her.

"I'm going to help you *boys* find more comfortable seating." She grabbed the man's thumb and twisted it over to his forearm.

"Ow, bitch, what do you think you're doing?" He tried to wrench his hand free but she applied more pressure.

"Now, unless you want me to shatter your wrist, which I'd be happy to do, you might want to move." For emphasis, she bored down until he stumbled into the aisle.

"I'm callin' the cops." His face had turned red.

"That's a good idea, let's call the security too. I'm sure they'll want to check yours and your bud's tickets."

"Never mind. Just let me go."

As she released him, she reached for the other man, who was already backing across the feet of the people seated farther down the row. "Lady, you're whacked."

Leaving the first chair open, she slowly sank into the second. She really hated drawing attention to herself like that, but it couldn't be helped. Those bubbas were in her seats and she had to be there—waiting. They'd picked the wrong day to mess with her. *I bet Janko is laughing his ass off. Geez, I wouldn't put it past him to have planted those two buttholes as a way to test me.*

A tall girl on the court caught her attention. She watched her zigzag between defenders to score an easy lay-up, then waved to a cheering woman near the sidelines. KC's heart tightened. *That could have been Ashley, and I could be here watching her play, not playing a waiting game.*

****

She was so close he could smell her. Just like he'd remembered. He inhaled her special fragrance and lust surged through his veins. If he reached out he could touch her, hold her, make her his. His fingers trembled, his belly quaked, his soft erection throbbed.

He licked his lips as he watched her walk down the

aisle to the seats he'd selected for them. Oh, he liked the way she handled the seat squatters and the pain she so easily meted out. A pleasurable tingle centered in his now rock hard penis as he imagined her, a small whip in her hand, rough riding him until he came. Of course, she'd have to let him play his games, too.

A loud cough shattered his fantasy. *Damn. Where was Delacourt and the girl?*

Almost time.

And time was on his side. He expelled an audible breath. If he had one, he could have the other. It wouldn't be long until his dream was complete.

****

Concentrating on the basketball game was useless, so KC scanned the crowd, focusing on individual faces. Who was she looking for? A raspy chuckle escaped through her clenched teeth. Two months ago during Tyler's baseball practice, Randy had bumped into her and apologized before he'd noticed who she was. Okay, maybe that wasn't fair as he only had eyes for the young mothers present, but still it made her pause. Would her pursuer recognize her?

She waited until the next game started before heading for the concession stand. As she passed into the lobby, the tiny hairs on the back of her neck spiked and goose bumps rose on her arms. Someone was watching her. Was he biding his time until...

Resisting the urge to spin about to find the person whose eyes were burning a hole in her back was hard. Instead, she eased into the concession stand crowd, plastering a cheerleader fake smile on her face. She had a case of the nerves but she'd be damned if she'd show it.

"Diet Coke, please." Her hand shook as she reached for a dollar bill, but steadied as she elbowed the polymer gun inside the waistband of her shorts. Tossing the bill on the counter, she grabbed the cup, sloshing some of the beverage on the floor as she turned.

Now was the perfect time to make a move on her, she

thought as she forced her cement feet to take one ponderous step after another down the populated concourse. She assessed the faces around her for signs of threats. Through the cacophony, she heard him closing in on her from behind. His footsteps rang out like shotgun blasts.

Be calm.

She transferred her drink to her left hand and kept walking. Her breathing slowed to normal. She was even able to smile at the security guard posted by the exit.

On her left, sets of metal doors burst open, releasing a flood of people into the lobby, making her go with them or be trampled. From the corner of her eye, she saw a familiar face in the crowd, and for that fraction of a second, she didn't want to believe that it was him. His moustache was lighter, but he still dyed his hair raven black. Her stomach lurched. He'd always cast a pall over her. That totally accounted for the creepiness she'd experienced earlier.

The afternoon sun broke from behind the clouds, filling the glass-enclosed concourse with more glare than light, and when she shaded her eyes, he was gone. She hadn't realized she'd been holding her breath until it came out with a whoosh. Gulping, she forced the rat's nest of emotions from her mind.

As she stepped through the doorway, the arena darkened and she paused as her eyes adjusted. On the court, she could see cheerleaders performing. She thought about Ashley and her heart compressed. Ashley was—is— a cheerleader, and a natural athlete, so good at everything she does. How was she handling her ordeal? *Probably a lot better than I am.*

A hand came down hard on her shoulder, steel fingers gripped, then yanked her backwards. Time slowed to nanoseconds as she heard her cup hit the ground and the man in the aisle seat curse. As she spun into the offending arm, her right foot connected with an instep.

Another curse.

Years of training became instinct as she sought to neutralize her attacker. She groped for a hold with her right hand as she drew back her left hand, palm up, then thrust it forward, striking flesh.

Arms, like bands of iron, hauled her against a broad male chest, knocking the air from her lungs.

"Is this your idea of foreplay?" His moustache tickled her ear, sending chills down her spine. She rested her head on his shoulder, allowing her body to melt into his in total surrender. Only his tight hold on her kept her from collapsing on the floor.

When she was finally able to draw a breath, she looked at him.

"Damn you, Janko. I coulda killed you. And I still might, you prick. What insanity made you scare me like that?" All at the same time, she was nail spitting angry with him, with herself for being caught off guard, and relieved that he was by her side. She placed her hand on his face, her thumb lightly caressing his mustached lip.

He kissed her palm, then placed his arm across her shoulder. "Have you seen anything? I've been scanning the crowds since we arrived. If he's here, he's good—real good. We're done for the day."

****

From the darkness of his hiding place, he watched the scene between Janko and KC. When they kissed, his body tensed, and grew hot as a murderous rage consumed him. He could end it all right here. Right now. The gun was already drawn, at home in his hand. Too loud, too messy, and too much of a chance I'll be caught, he thought as he slipped the pistol back into the holster.

Damn that fuckin' Janko. Bastard. Why was he with KC? How had he found her? From that moron Delacourt. Bet Dumb Del didn't even have her or the girl when he checked in yesterday. If Janko hadn't killed him, the man would. There would be no great loss, Delacourt was going to end up dead anyway.

As for Janko, he'd take his own sweet time killing

him, not too fast, but inch-by-inch, starting with that face that all women thought so damn handsome. The man would savor each and every pleasurable moment as he made Janko atone for all the sins that bastard had committed against him.

When Janko put his arm around KC, she smiled at him, and the man wanted to smash her face in. She'd never smiled at him like that. Whore. Wanting Janko when she could have him. The unworthy bitch would pay dearly for yet another betrayal with that bastard.

Plans for revenge permeated his mind. Somehow, someway, he'd take from her what she'd taken from him. She'd lose what she loved most in this world, and he'd make her watch. Then, he'd make her beg him to end her life.

His hands fisted, aching to pound mercilessly on something—anything. Hate was good. It fueled him. Gave him an edge.

He shadowed the couple as they exited the building. They may have thought they'd won this round, but they weren't as smart as he was. No one could match his superior intelligence.

****

A short time later, Janko and KC sat on a tree-shaded covered patio, two bottles of cold beer sweating on the scarred wooden table. A basket of chips sat untouched next to a cup of salsa. She'd grown quiet on the short ride over, and he chalked it up to fatigue. They *had* spent most of the night in each other's arms. He took a long swig from his beer, then let his gaze roam. The small Mexican restaurant had just enough *tourista* décor, with colorful serapes and pottery adorning the walls, piñatas hanging from rough wooden beams and terrazzo tiled floors. Red vinyl booths, patched with duct tape, lined three walls while tile-topped tables filled the middle. Lazy moving ceiling fans circulated the air, mixing the fresh herbs and flowers in planter boxes that decorated the adobe patio wall with the delicious aromas from the kitchen. His stomach grumbled, reminding him they hadn't eaten all day. The food served was pure Tex-Mex, the best in Austin. He'd had a hard time deciding what to order. Holding up the bottle, he caught the attention of the only waitress. "*Dos cervasas, por favor.*"

She returned with their beer, food, and hot corn tortillas. The smell of chilies and beef surrounded them. He released a *tamale* from its steaming husk and was tempted to take that first savory bite, but he knew better than to get burned by his impatience. That's how he had to handle KC. She was tempting, delicious, and if he allowed his desires to show too much, she'd burn him.

Picking up a tortilla from the stack, he smeared on butter followed by a couple of shakes of salt before rolling it and taking a bite. The warm butter coated his lips just as KC had last night. He could still feel the satiny smoothness of her skin as he caressed every inch of her, the way her body trembled when he teased and tasted until she was at the edge of climax, then sliding into her tight warmth. She'd satisfied a hunger within him that no one else could. Was making love with her going to be one of those infrequent treats, like real Austin Tex-Mex, that he could only have when the timing was right? God, he hoped not.

Reaching for a chip, he became aware of her watching him. In the subdued light, her eyes were more green than brown, with that spark that made him forget everything but getting inside her.

"I did see someone today—my father."

Her softly spoken words caught him by surprise. Half of a chip filled with salsa burned as it slid down his throat. Grabbing the long-neck, he tipped up the bottle, hoping the beer would soothe the fire inside. He swallowed hard, then swallowed again as the lump in his throat dislodged. "How do you know it was him and not someone else?"

She shrugged. "I can still recognize my own father."

Breaking the remaining chips in the basket, she

appeared detached. He couldn't remember a time when she'd ever been this calm where her father was concerned. She had, and always would, blame him for her mother's sudden death. He blamed Patrick for teaching her not to trust men. Hell, he hadn't done a real good job himself with her either. "And you didn't think that was important enough to tell me at the center?"

"I think he was Delacourt's contact."

"Why?"

"He's not above this kind of trick to get what he covets."

He watched as a slow flush stained her cheeks. The fresh bloom of anger heightened her beauty and his body responded, making it difficult to keep his mind on business. It took him a few moments to mentally shift gears. "I'm not saying that he isn't involved somehow, but why use Delacourt?"

"Could my father be connected with the agency?"

"No."

"I want to make sure. Let's go pay *Daddy* a little visit." She rose, not waiting for him as he tossed money on the table to cover the check.

He found her using the totally unsophisticated low-tech method of the telephone book to find Patrick, then stood by as she called.

A sly grin slowly played on her lips as he heard a voice on the line answer. She hung up the phone, then let out a deep sigh. "He's home."

****

The thought of seeing her father again made KC's stomach hurt. It didn't make sense why he'd only want to see Ashley and not Tyler, but if he *was* the one threatening her children, she'd kill him without prejudice.

Janko drove as she watched for the signs to Onion Creek.

The night seemed to close in on her soul. The massive trees along the winding road bent and swayed as if to say "Go back." In the distance, she heard an owl hoot three times. Her mother had always told her that owls were messengers of death. Well, maybe she was the messenger this time.

A tall iron fenced separated Onion Creek Estates from the highway, and she'd expected more of a secure gated community as they passed the empty guard booth. Two rows of antique reproduction streetlights stood sentry, their blue glow abruptly stopping when the road split around a massive oak. The car's headlights illuminated a directional sign.

"Which way?" He slowed the car.

"Since he lives on Birdie Drive, follow the arrows to the golf course."

The course was in the center of the sprawling complex, and identical limestone duplexes flanked both sides of the street. While searching for the right house number, she noticed that even the landscaping was the same. It must be rough on the residents if they were having a bad day and couldn't remember where they lived. Kind of a nasty trick to pull on old people, she thought cynically.

"There it is." She pointed to a house on the course side of the street as they slowly passed by. He continued on, then turned off the headlights before circling back to park the car next to Patrick's house.

Time to face fears. She took a deep breath, exhaling in a chuff before getting out. Janko's silence, his tacit approval, let her know he'd follow her lead. His trust was empowering and what she required right now.

She took his hand in hers as they walked toward her father's home. The foreboding that had blanketed her earlier faded as a sense of rightness spread like Janko's warmth by her side. They looked like a couple out for an evening stroll on the golf course, and in a strange way, she wished it was so.

Stopping in the shadow of a tree, she tugged him into her, and kissed him hard, possessively, hotly, as if her very essence demanded it. When he leaned in, trapping her between the tree trunk and his erection, she rubbed against him as her aching need hurt more than the rough bark gouging her back. This was madness, but she wanted his touch—to feel something good before confronting the bad.

He broke the kiss as he shifted his weight slightly, leaving her body, and her mind, to cool. Cupping his bottom, she didn't release him until her pulsing core eased.

"Now what?" His words came out low and husky.

"Time to chase away the shadows."

"Are you sure?" He kissed her forehead. She'd never been more sure of anything in her life as her gaze briefly lifted to his.

Crossing the grassy expanse, the light from Patrick's unit helped her skirt lawn furniture until she reached his patio. With the curtains pulled back, she had an unrestricted view of the living room. When she held up her hand, Janko stood motionless behind her, his breath fanning wisps of her hair as they watched for movement. His presence meant more than someone covering her backside. It was potent. Forceful. Comforting. But she would be damned before she admitted that to him.

Reaching for the door handle, she fleetingly hesitated before firmly grasping the cool brass. It turned readily, then she noiselessly pushed the door open. She stood a few feet inside her father's house, feeling like the intruder that she was. She'd had no home since her mother died.

Glancing around the room, she crinkled her nose at the polished professional decorator touch that screamed money and lack of personal taste. The black, white and gray color scheme repeated in every detail. A charcoal leather couch and love seat flanked a black and white geometric area rug, creating an optical illusion of depth on the thick, dove gray wall-to-wall carpet. Stylized chrome lamps sprouted misshapen appendages with shrouded lights, guaranteed no doubt to flatter the aging Patrick.

On her left an Art Deco bar, complete with the soda shop barstools, divided the kitchen from the living room. The black and white checkered design, from the tile counters to the floor, made her groan. A splash of color drew her attention to the right where she recognized a Warhohl of her father. Shaking her head in disgust, she knew that her father couldn't tell the difference between a Monet and a Picasso, and cared only about the impression his art made on others. In the corner, a freestanding fireplace sat on gray slate tiles, cold like the rest of the room.

The soft crooning of Andy Williams crept into her awareness, and sadness filled her along with the song. He'd been her mother's favorite singer. Directly across the room, a black lacquer entertainment center took up most of the wall, but the music surrounded the room.

A fresh wave of nostalgia washed over her as she looked for something familiar, something from her childhood. Had Patrick kept anything from when they were a family? She'd promised herself a long time ago that he'd never hurt her again, so why was there a catch in her heart?

From down the dark hallway, a door closed and she heard him singing Moon River, his tenor voice warbling with age. He entered the living room without seeing her, so she used the clandestine moments to examine him. His maroon silk pajamas complimented his tanned skin and close-cropped dark hair. He'd maintained his trim physique, probably from playing golf everyday, or chasing after women.

Apprehension constricted her lungs. It'd been so long and not long enough, since she'd spoken to him. Only to preserve the welfare of her children was she here. This was for them. Steeling herself, she forced her voice to stay even. "You're still flying your 19th hole flag. Is the bar open?"

"Oh Lord have mercy!" He clutched his chest as he stumbled back into the wall, his eyes widening in recognition. "Angel baby." As he looked past her to Janko, he jumped. "Where's the girl? Don't think you're getting any more of my money without producing my granddaughter. T'wasn't part of the bargain." His face discolored as he waved an accusing finger. "No, you'll not be seeing another dime of it."

He headed for the tall black cabinet next to the painting. When he pulled the top section of doors, KC reached for her gun until she realized that he'd opened a bar. The light turned the crystal ware on the glass shelves into prisms that shot color into the room. Decanters with engraved silver collars were filled with liquor. Patrick grabbed three tumblers and poured a hefty measure of Scotch each. He took a glass, drained it, then refilled it before he turned around. "Drink? No? Suit yourself."

Closing the distance between them, he leaned on the sofa back, his gaze raking her. When she was little, he had the power to strip her with only a look, making her feel dirty and ashamed. She suppressed a shudder, refusing to bend under his scrutiny and returned his stare with one of her own. When he shrunk back, she smiled inwardly at her own power over her father.

"I'm not your little girl anymore, *Father*. I grew up real quick when you tried to play your 'games' with me. I always knew when you were watching me. My flesh would crawl, like it did today at the basketball playoffs. And when you'd bump into me, or brush your body against mine, don't think that I didn't know what you were doing. Its called covert incest. Mother knew, and protected me the best she could, but you took your frustration out on her. I saw the scars, the bruises, even though she tried to hide them. I escaped by joining the agency, and Mother— by dying."

"Oh, Angel baby, is that what you really think?" His condescending tone infuriated her.

Crossing to the entertainment center, she clicked off the stereo before turning to the bookshelves. She fingered a few of the small knickknacks, then absently ran a fingernail across the expanse of book spines a few times, enjoying the clacking noise that filled the silent room. Pivoting slowly, she waited until his gaze rose to hers.

"Did you know the agency made me into an efficient killing machine? Did you know that's what your little girl grew up to be? Someone who gets paid to get rid of scum like you." Her voice was cutting, her words deliberately cruel from the years of hurt and hate.

The thick carpet muffled the few steps she took toward him. Holding up her hand, she grinned, as his eyes grew large and wary. "I've got all I need right here to kill you before you can blink, and the authorities will simply think that an old man like you had a heart attack. Don't kid yourself that I won't hurt you because you're my father. I want some answers and I want them now. I'll make you talk, one way or the other. The choice is yours. Who were you supposed to meet at the Erwin Center?"

He paled as he looked between her and Janko. "I—I was to meet him, and he'd let me see you and Ashley."

The firm rein on her anger slipped and she exploded, seizing her father by his pajama top, the crystal glass flying from his hand to shatter against the wall. Inches separated them. He reeked of liquor and fear as she twisted the silk fabric ever tighter around his neck. "How do you know about Ashley? Tell me, or I swear...I'll kill you right now."

"Let him go, KC."

"Stay out of this." Janko's hand was on her arm, and she jerked away, pulling Patrick off balance toward her. Not wanting any more contact with him than was necessary, she shoved him over the sofa where he crumpled in a heap.

He gasped, once, twice, sucking air into his lungs, while he struggled to sit up. She watched dispassionately as a coughing fit seized him and his bony shoulders convulsed until his breathing steadied. When he faced her, she saw how incredibly old he'd become with his rheumy eyes, deep wrinkles on his face, and excess skin that sagged around his neck like a collar.

"I just wanted to see my granddaughter," he wheezed.

KC gaped at him, biting back the words she longed to hurl. *The hell you'll ever see my kids.* Then it hit her that he'd mentioned only his granddaughter and not grandson. If he knew about Ashley, why didn't he know about Tyler?

"I guess you had your reasons not to let me be a part of your life," his voice trailed low. "But when *your* friend here," he nodded at Janko, "called last week wanting to know if I had your address, I got jealous and wanted to see you, too. I've missed you, Angel baby."

She glanced over her shoulder to look at Janko.

"It wasn't me." He'd moved to lean against the kitchen bar, his legs casually crossed at the ankles, his expression nonchalant. "I've always known where you were."

She wanted to believe him, but a worm of doubt crawled inside her. He'd betrayed her before, and lying came so damn easy for him. Hurt slivered her heart. If he'd known, he'd never bothered to see her.

With a great amount of effort, Patrick rose from the couch, his shoulders bowed. A slight tremor shook his age spotted hand as he pointed a finger at Janko. "The caller identified himself as you and we made a deal. Every man has his price, even you." He used the back of the couch for support as his unsteady legs brought him closer to her. "I was to give him your address and a fifty thousand dollar deposit for him to bring you and Ashley to Austin, then I'd pay him the other fifty."

"Chump change, old man." Janko folded his arms, a smug look tattooed on his face. "You've been had."

"But—but, Kelly," he stammered as he pleaded his case to her, "you've got to understand that was the only way I knew to be able to see you both. You'd never come if I asked."

"Damn right. Do you think I'd ever allow my children to get near you? And what you tried to do is kidnapping—

a federal offense." She massaged her temples as she sorted out the confusion. "How did you know where I lived?"

"Your mother. I was moving a few things around when I found an old letter she'd tucked inside her Bible. It was from Ashley. The envelope had a return address label with your name. I was getting ready to hire a private investigator when I got his phone call. Angel—"

She held up her hand, motioning him to stop. Queasiness struck her like a rock as she remembered an eight-year-old Ashley asking a million questions about the grandmother she'd never known. KC had just come in from tending a sick foal and had been in the kitchen trying to fix dinner. While Tyler sat underneath her feet banging on pots and lids with wooden spoons, Ashley had quizzed her on why she couldn't see her other grandmother. In a harried mother's way, she'd given her daughter a lame answer. *Tenacious child. Ashley must have searched her closet until she found some of Mother's old letters she couldn't part with.*

Inhaling, she held it briefly before expelling it, willing herself to calm down. "So what were you going to do after you saw us at the Erwin Center?"

"Try to persuade you to stay for a few days. I'm a sick old man—"

"Sick is right!" With hands on hips, she scowled at him.

"Where was the exchange to be made?" Janko's voice sliced through the tension.

"We...In the parking lot." He looked first at Janko, then at her. "It was a set up, wasn't it?"

Janko unfolded his arms. "Looks that way."

KC watched as her father's head drooped momentarily, then quickly rose.

"I've been played for a fool." His gaze, fiery and sharp, centered on her, and she stepped back as he walked toward her until her heel struck the baseboard. The hair on her nape prickled. He stopped at the bookcase, removed a leather bound Bible, then flipped it open. Standing directly in front of her, he tilted the book so she could read an envelope with her mother's name scrawled by a child—her child. A heart shaped gold locket and chain lay in the crease.

"Your mother wanted Ashley to have this. The locket was from her grandmother. There's a note."

As she started to take it from him, she knocked over a figurine, and the noise made her jump.

Suddenly, Patrick had flattened her against the wall, his body touching every inch of hers. "I love you," he said as he took her with him to the floor.

"Get off me." She used both hands to shove him away as she scrambled out from beneath him. Janko grabbed under her arms, dragging her into the kitchen as the thump of a bullet buried in the wall where her head had been.

"KC. Are you hit?" He crouched by her side, his body shielding hers as he wiped her face.

She stared first at his bloody hands, then her own as she sat up. "No."

"Angel?" Her father's voice sounded far away. When she tried to crawl to him, Janko caught her foot.

"Let me go," she said as she kicked free. Kneeling beside her father, she saw the dark stain spreading from the fist size hole in his chest. She knew there was nothing she could do for him now and pushed a lock of hair from his face.

Patrick's eyelids fluttered and he tried to lift his hand. As she took it in hers, he gave her a bittersweet smile, frothy blood pooling in the corners of his mouth. "I real-ly love you. To see you...one last time." He labored to get each word out with slow shallow breaths.

"Oh, Father." She gripped his hand tighter as his went slack. "I love you, too."

"KC, I'm sorry, he's DRT. We've gotta move. You're still in danger." Janko, his gun drawn, tugged at her shirt.

She looked at Janko as if she'd never seen him before. He'd used such a callous term—DRT—dead right there, and twenty minutes ago, she'd have said the same. But not now. She placed Patrick's hand by his side, then closed his eyes. For so long she hadn't acknowledged that he existed and now that he was gone, she felt cheated. Robbed of what should have been the perfect parents, the perfect childhood, the perfect family.

"KC."

Before getting up, she noticed her mother's Bible against the wall. She tried to pick it up, but the bloody leather slipped from her hand. Janko threw her a kitchen towel and she carefully wrapped the book, then tucked it under her arm. As she and Janko crept to the front door, she said a silent goodbye to her father, grateful to have made peace with him.

Chapter Eight

Janko motioned for KC to stay on the darkened front porch as he slipped around the corner of the house. Scanning the adjacent yards, he watched for movement, or the odd shadow that didn't belong. As he crept between the condo and the golf course, he berated himself for not anticipating the attempt on her life. Maybe he was getting as soft as he'd accused her of becoming. He'd let them both down.

From inside one of the condos, he heard a dog barking. When the outside light came on, he used the shrubbery to conceal his crouched walk to a group of small trees where he thought the shooter had been. How had that bastard found them? Were they counter-surveilled? He'd wagered their lives they hadn't been followed, and he'd almost lost her with that bet. From across the yard, he noted the line of fire into the living room had been a clean shot. Patrick's death was no accident.

He took a step when something hard rolled under his shoe. Moving slightly, he picked up a brass casing. "Too sloppy," he said as he put the spent round in his pocket. "Way too sloppy."

Hurrying back to KC, he wrapped his body around hers as they sprinted for the car. If the sniper were still around, which he doubted, he'd not allow her to be an easy target. Locking the car could either be a godsend or a blunder, but he'd take the chance the shooter wasn't inside. The dome light shone like a beacon when he opened the door. As he shoved her across the front seat, he scanned the back, a measure of relief flowing through him when he saw nothing. He quietly closed his door, but the light remained on until he turned the key.

"Stay down." As much as he wanted to speed away, he eased the darkened car down the street. The noise from the tires moving at a slug-slow pace were amplified by the night air and grated against his already frayed nerves. Not attracting undue attention from the neighbors *or* the sniper was paramount. He could afford no more surprises tonight. Once past the golf course, he resumed a normal speed until he reached the highway.

Merging with the Saturday night traffic, he used it to his advantage as he performed a few evasive maneuvers. The quick lane changes bounced her from the seat to the floorboard like a rag doll. "You can sit up now, we're in the clear. You okay?"

"Oh, yeah. Peachy after getting sniped then pulverized by your driving. Just like old times, huh?"

Her voice was even, sarcastic, and made him smile. She'd been through a lot, and might be shaken, but she'd bounce back. When the game got rough, she got tougher.

As the air circulated in the car, he caught the faint scent of her perfume and drew in a deeper breath. The lights on the highway illuminated the inside of the car, so he stole a glimpse at her. His gut clenched at her composure and the way she held her head high. He'd never been prouder of her, or wanted her as much as he did right now.

He focused his attention back on the road by counting the dotted lines until they blurred into one. When she finally broke the silence, he found himself gripping the steering wheel so hard his knuckles had whitened.

"Why was Patrick taken out?" Her matter-of-fact tone was just that, like the way they talked during a debriefing.

"He got in the way."

"He saved my life."

"He gave you up." His voice was as devoid of emotion as hers.

The scene at Patrick's played in his mind like an old videotape—fuzzy and yellow. From the time he'd internalized the plink against the glass as a shot, he'd reacted in slow motion, as if his body was moving through molasses as he advanced toward KC. He could see his arms reaching for her as he shouted. His words, slurred and thick, had sounded as if they came from a tape recorder with run down batteries.

Did he have any right to blame Patrick for almost getting her killed? Or did the blame belong solely to him because he doomed those he loved the most? He reminded himself that he couldn't love her, and what he churned inside was merely caring. That's all.

His ribs ached as the staccato beat in his chest increased. The ever-widening pool of blood as it stained the carpet swam before his eyes. The surge of terror that she'd been hit swept over him again. He broke into a cold sweat. Love hurt. But where he was concerned, love killed.

****

KC processed what Janko had said. She hated it when he was right. Patrick, even though he'd meant only to see her again, had led the killer right to her, and he'd paid for his mistake with his life. What had been her mistake that made someone come after her and Ashley?

Restless, she needed to occupy her mind when it slowly dawned on her that the weight in her lap had grown heavier. Her hands rested on top of the towel-covered Bible. Even through the darkness, she could see the outline of bloodstains on the fabric.

She reached for the reading lamp on the rear view mirror, fumbling with the switch until Janko helped her. Across the car, she read his questioning look before he gave her a go-ahead nod. As she focused her attention on peeling away the terry cloth, loops had stuck to the fine leather and she had to rub to get them off. Balls of cotton, blood and gold flecked her fingers as she wiped the cover clean. Her hand trembled when she found the bullet hole through the embossed title.

Saved by "The Good Book." She tried to open it, but the blood and the bullet had fused the pages. Wedging her fingers between the sheets, she freed the section where the locket rested, and on the other side, a metal slug poked from the page.

She pried the bullet loose, then held the silver mushroom shape in her palm. "This killed my fa-ther," her voice cracked, "and it damn near killed me."

Janko did a double take. He sent the car careening across two lanes of traffic to the shoulder, then braked so hard the tires skidded on the loose gravel. Slamming the car in park, he dug in his pants pocket and pulled out a shell casing.

"What's wrong with you?" The slug danced as if it had come back to life. She trapped it between her fingers.

"KC, we got him. I know who made this bullet." Holding it where she could see, he turned it first one way, then the other as the lights from passing cars glinted off the brass. "Let me have that." He stretched out his hand and she dropped the spent round in it.

"Looks like an ordinary .308 round to me." He handed her the brass.

"See the mark on the casing rim? It's a head stamp. An infinity head stamp. I didn't notice it at first because I thought the hammer had left scratches, but the color of the slug did it. There's only one ammunition maker in the world that signs his custom loads with an infinity mark."

She tipped the casing, and there in the dim light, the lazy 8 figure appeared. A sad smile tugged at her mouth as she turned to him.

He cupped her face, then kissed her hard. When he drew back, she saw pride shining in his eyes. "You're something else, KC. We gonna nail that son-of a-bitch."

After he'd let her go, she sank back in her seat, gawking at him. A little bit of his Louisiana heritage had slipped out, along with a rare display of genuine emotion, and for the first time since she'd left Oklahoma, she had a glimmer of hope.

Shifting the car into gear, he spun the tires then sped to the next exit where he took the turn on two wheels. She gripped the armrest.

"You seem to know where we're going. Want to let me in on it, too?"

He gave her a toothy grin. "New Orleans, to see a man about a bullet."

****

Janko breathed a little easier now, and he shifted in his seat. In less than an hour they were flying to New Orleans. Wonderful things...money and greed. Both had made it possible to rent the Cessna despite the late time. He had plenty of money, the man at the FBO had wanted a lot of it and they'd both left happy.

He'd hustled KC from the car into the plane without a word, done a fast preflight check, then taken off. She slumped in the seat, her stare—vacant as the Bates Motel—made him suspect that she'd checked out mentally as well as physically.

He rubbed the stubble on his jaw. The demands of the last few days taxed his physical stamina more than any mission ever had before.

The horizon met thick blue gray clouds that held back the first rays of dawn. By the time he'd landed the small plane, then rented a car, he'd reached his limit and wondered how much more he could go himself. His eyelids were like sandpaper, scraping his eyes as they closed, then again as he forced them open. The cramp in his foot snaked up into his calf, and his hands ached as he clutched the wheel. In his periphery, he noticed she'd succumbed to her exhaustion as her head bobbed like one of those plastic dogs on a car dashboard. Taking the next exit, he headed for a no-tell motel nestled in a seedier part of the French Quarter. He pulled up to the office, leaving the car running.

A bug splattered neon "vacancy" sign hummed and the screen door hinges creaked as he entered. Seeing no one, he tapped the bell several times, hoping it could be heard over the bellowing TV. A leather-faced woman in a stained housedress shuffled from a back room, a cigarette dangling precariously from the corner of her crinkled mouth. She quickly took his money, dropped a line of ashes when she handed him a key, then returned where she'd come from.

Back outside, he moved the car to the end of the building, parking a few feet away from their room. "Come on." He gently nudged KC, but she didn't move more than a few inches. When he got out, he slammed his door, thinking that might jolt her awake, but nope, she was still out. After opening her door, he unbuckled her seat belt. "I'll carry you over my shoulder like a sack of potatoes, if I have to."

Her eyelids stood fixed at half-staff when she rose. With the book cradled in both hands, she dragged her feet as he steered her to the room. He returned to the car for their bags and heard the springs screech as she collapsed on the bed. After checking the parking lot one more time, he entered the room, then secured the door with the chain and the flimsy knob lock. A weary groan escaped when he leaned against the door.

A small stream of sunshine slipped between the curtains, highlighting the worn purple shag, the scarred wooden dresser and a miniscule room that had seen better days forty years ago, but at least it was cleaner than he'd expected. Crossing to the sink, he dropped both bags, then looked left into the bathroom and debated on a shower or sleep first. Sleep won out.

With her arms and legs sprawled out and her feet hanging over the edge, KC had taken up almost all of the double bed. He removed her tennis shoes, letting them tumble to the floor before he sat. The mattress sagged under his weight. If she'd been sleeping on her side instead of her stomach, she'd have rolled into him. And that wouldn't have been so bad, he thought as he moved the hair from her face, his fingers lingering longer than was necessary.

The shadows under her eyes were bruise-dark against her skin pale. She looked fragile—vulnerable—in need of his protection. Was he reading too much into this situation? Had she come to him because she trusted him or because he could give her what she needed? Did she need him as much as he needed her?

I'm a few barks over dog-tired to come up with thoughts like that.

Stretching out on the small sliver of space she'd left, he balanced on the edge. When he couldn't get comfortable, he lifted her arm and placed it on his chest as he inched to the middle. She snuggled closer, letting out a contented sigh.

All too soon, Janko woke as sweat trickled down his neck. He'd forgotten to set the air conditioner and the afternoon sun had turned the room into an oven. His entire body, his clothes, even his pillow, was drenched. He smelled worse than a dirty gym sock.

A shower had now become a necessity. He eased off the bed, careful not to wake her, took a few steps, then doubled back to turn on the window unit. Hot air and dust spewed out as the ancient machine clunked three times, finally settling into a dull roar that alternated between the sound of a lawn mower and a chain saw. As he walked to the bathroom, he checked to see if the noise had woken her, but she hadn't stirred.

The ancient shower curtain crackled beneath his hand and the metal hooks screeched against the rusted rod when he pulled it back. Twisting both the hot and cold knobs, he grimaced as orange water trickled from a white-crusted showerhead into the tub. He rolled his eyes but continued peeling his sweat soaked clothes off. By the time he'd stripped, the water had cleared and was running fast enough to swirl around the corroded drain. He adjusted the temperature, but the water never got hotter than tepid. As long as it was wet, he thought wryly.

The spray, such as it was, cooled his body and he allowed his mind to shift into neutral. No thoughts. No threats. No problems.

A breeze bit his backside. He turned, his muscles coiled and ready. The shower curtain parted.

"How's the water?" Her voice was husky from sleep as she stepped in with him.

One side of her face was ruddy and still bore the mark from the seam of the pillowcase, while the other was smooth and perfect. God, she was beautiful. He moved slightly to allow the small jet of water to caress her, wishing it was his hands sliding down her satiny skin. "Glad you could join me."

"Hmmm." She motioned for him to face the water.

Reaching for the soap, she pressed her body against his, flattening her breasts on his back. Her warm and soapy hands rubbed brusquely over his chest, stopping briefly to tweak his nipples into tighter buds, then dipped lower to lather the hair around his growing arousal.

A groan of pure pleasure escaped him. She nibbled on his shoulder as she continued exploring his body. The water misted over them like a light spring rain. His resolve to stay away from her weakened with every stroke of her soapy hands. Closing his eyes, he remembered long ago when she'd been part of him.

He missed her. Missed her touch. Missed the way she made his senses key whenever she was near. It would be so easy for him to fall in love with her again and dream about forever. But he'd have to relinquish his heart.

Whispering, he told her his carnal intentions, then lightly nibbled on her neck. Her body quivered momentarily before she tensed.

"Hey, watch what you're strangling down there." He managed a light falsetto voice as she giggled. "You think that's funny, don't you?" Turning around, he held her face between his hands and watched her smile fade.

"Steven? I need you. I... "

The water continued to sluice down their bodies as he peered into her eyes. They were clear, without a trace of hesitation, without sadness. He read trust and confidence in them, too.

His lips claimed her mouth, and he swept his tongue inside. She tasted of honey and a raw aching passion. Pressing his body against her, he gently slid into her tight warmth, almost losing his load. With just a few strokes, he...

"Babe," he murmured as he withdrew. Stepping over the tub ledge, he helped her out only to sweep her off her feet and carry her to the bed. He laid her down, spreading her damp hair over a pillow, then watched as the cool air raised goose bumps on her skin and her nipples puckered into rosy peaks. Bending his head, he suckled first one, then the other. He trailed his tongue down her belly as his fingers rolled her fleshy nub until it crested. Her body quivered with each of his tender touches and she pressed against his hand, her soft throaty moans increasing to guttural cries.

Her entreaties, born of lust and longing, fueled his desire as he lifted her hips, then possessively slipped into her. She greedily matched his passion stroke for stroke until she arched, screaming out his name. His excitement grew as she rolled him to his back, then straddled him. Slowly, gently, she gloved him and he closed his eyes, reveling in the intense overwhelming pleasures. Her muscular thighs gripped his hips, increasing the friction as she rode him. He knew his control was slipping. When she came again, the tattered vestiges of his will disintegrated, and he filled her.

Drawing her to him, he held her until her shudders subsided and their heartbeats slowed. Her hair fell around them like a golden curtain, and he was surrounded by the flowery fragrance that belonged to her alone. Utterly content, he knew she was the only woman who'd ever touched the part of him that made him feel whole, alive. He kissed her tenderly, not wanting the moment to end.

"I've missed you so much." Her voice, as smoky as her eyes, warmed him.

"Me, too." Oh God, he had.

Bunching a pillow under her head, she started to cover up with the bedspread, when he stopped her. Propped on one elbow, he pushed her hair behind her ears, then ran a finger down her nose and across her mouth. She drew his finger inside, lightly sucking on it, sending currents that pulsed through his body.

If he'd been younger, there would be no doubt he'd have her sitting astride him right now. Extracting his finger from her mouth, he circled her nipple and left a shiny wet trail. His hand slid across her belly, but stopped abruptly when he touched the small round scar. The tips of his fingers explored the old wound.

"What happened here?"

"Just a memento from a failed relationship."

"Your husband didn't do this, did he?" He leaned over to run his tongue over the puckered skin, kissed it, then laid his head on her stomach.

Her laugh was taut, brittle. "Ex-husband? No, not his style."

"Why aren't you still with him?" A spark of jealousy flicked through him as he thought about her with another man. It was masochistic, but he had to know about the man that had taken his place, touched her, made love to her, given her children, and been stupid enough to let her go.

KC ran her fingers through his hair, then smoothed the sweat dampened locks from his temple. She didn't want to think, or talk, only to ride out the sensations that his lovemaking had given her.

He shifted to look at her. "Are you going to answer me?"

She squirmed under his inquisitive gaze. "We don't really want to talk about him, do we?"

"One of us does."

"Let's just say it didn't work out." She gave his hair a gentle tug. "Okay?"

"How long were you married?" From the look in his eyes, she knew he wasn't going to drop the subject.

"Almost five years. I met Randy shortly after leaving Pegasus." She shrugged. Randy was the last person she ever wanted to talk about, especially to Janko. Nothing good would come of this discussion, only bad memories.

"Where?"

Turning her head so she couldn't see him, she paused a moment to collect her thoughts. "Treaty Hill. It's a typical small town, with typical small town ways."

"As in everyone knows your business."

"Yes, but in this close-knit community, unless you're related to someone in one way or another, strangers aren't accepted."

The faces of the elderly couple who'd taken her in appeared from her memory. Years making a living farming were etched in the deep creases of their leathery skin. Their hands were gnarled and arthritic from hard work, yet gentle. They'd stumbled across her in a roadside park in west Texas, taken pity, brought her into their home to heal, and changed her life. "The elderly couple I stayed with told everyone I was the granddaughter of an old friend. And since Esther and Lloyd were his aunt and uncle, I couldn't keep from running into him."

"But why did you marry him?"

Because you didn't give a damn if I dropped off the face of the earth. Because I thought I could forget you if I allowed him into my life. Because it was the best thing for me to do.

She glared at Janko. "He gave me a place to live, a chance to make a new life, and a new career raising kids and horses." *After the first two months, I knew we weren't right for each other. He wasn't you.*

Janko stared at her. Silent empty moments drifted by before he spoke. "And the rest of the story?"

"Then one day, he told me I'd changed because I no

longer looked the other way when he came home drunk, or when he slept around. He said I didn't give him the proper respect due a man. He divorced me, but..." Her voice dwindled, "You're never rid of them when kids are involved."

KC shut her eyes as she remembered the last day she'd seen Randy. He'd stormed into her house while she'd been retrieving her gun from the top shelf of her walk-in closet.

"What the hell is going on? Where are Ashley and Tyler?" he'd shouted as he blocked her from leaving.

"Randy, I don't have time to explain, but I'm going to get them back."

"What makes you think you can? You're only—"

"A woman?" She tried to push him out of the way, but he stood like an oak.

"Answer me, Kelly." He took off his ball cap and wiped his brow with his forearm.

"Because of what I used to do." She shoved her fist into his meaty chest as she passed, but he grabbed her, his fingers digging deep into her left bicep.

In less than a blink, she brought her .38 to rest between his eyes. The metallic slam of the hammer echoed as it struck an empty chamber.

She watched the intricate play of shock and horror cross his face, then she lowered the gun and yanked out of his grasp. Stopping at the bed, she bristled as his wide-eyed gaze bore into her, but calmly flicked open the gun's cylinder with her thumb.

While she loaded the malevolent looking hollow point bullets into the Smith and Wesson, she heard the loud release of his pent up breath.

"M—my God. W—what did you used to do?"

She turned to face him. Click. Snip. Snap. She slapped the cylinder into a spin, then put the revolver in her gear bag. "Kill people." She read the fear in his eyes. And she'd savored the brief moment, but the victory had been hollow.

A tear slipped down KC's cheek and Janko's warm lips pressed against the wetness.

"Oh, babe," he uttered softly as he cradled her.

She wasn't sad about what was, but what could have been. Should have been with Janko.

Opening her eyes, she sought his reaction. If she'd been expecting sympathy, it wasn't there in his blue eyes. Only fiery, unquenchable passion. She licked her lips and he greedily claimed them. He made her hot and needy, shaky and weak. Her hand slipped around his growing erection, where she stroked, kneaded and tweaked, his groans spurring her on. Guiding him, she rubbed herself along his length, not allowing him to penetrate.

"You're driving me crazy," he growled, his voice a mixture of ragged frustration and yearning.

"Want me to stop?"

He punctuated his crude remark by snatching her under him. The rasp of his chest hair across her sensitive nipples sent tingles all the way to her toes. It was now his turn to tease and torment her. With his knee, he nudged her thighs apart as he oh-so-slowly entered and withdrew from her again and again, ignoring her pleas to stay inside. Infinitesimally, he increased the pace as well as the friction as she teetered on the edge of release. When he took her completely, she climaxed fast and hard, her muscles grasping him deeply, welcoming his seed.

His eyes remained closed until his spasms quit, and when he did open them, he smiled that sleepy satisfied smirk that warmed her heart. Her body still throbbed around him. A sense of rightness enveloped her that she wanted to scream she loved him.

Always had.

Always would.

Even though she now lay in his arms, their physical parting sent a chill over her. "We need to talk..."

As he began to snore, the golden glow that had encompassed her fled as if an inflated balloon had slipped away before it could be tied.

Oh, gee thanks, Steven! No 'wow, that was great, KC.' Or 'thanks for the incredible sex, KC.' Or 'how 'bout them Lakers?'

What had she expected? For him to confess his undying love? Never. That wasn't his way. In the years they had been together, he'd never once told her he loved her. So why would he start now? Because she longed for him to. She ached to be as important to him as he was to her.

When he relaxed his grip, she stole from his embrace and saw the outline of their wet bodies on the bedspread. The room smelled of hot sweaty sex, and so did she.

After taking a shower, she slipped on his T-shirt just like she used to. Her memory of some things had faded over the years, but she'd never forgotten that he'd been the best—and the worst—thing that had ever happened to her. And if she wasn't careful, he'd break her heart again.

On the corner of the dresser, she spied the fine gold chain dangling from the pages of her mother's Bible. Walking over, she eased out the locket. The once rounded surface had caved in with the bullet's impact, and the clasp permanently sprung, leaving the locket half open. Inside, she saw a yellowed picture of her mother, father and herself.

If her mother hadn't wanted Ashley to have the locket... if her father hadn't given her the Bible... if he hadn't pulled her to the ground... She was grateful to them for giving her life, and grateful to them for saving her life.

Grateful to have escaped death for a chance to repair her life.

Maybe Janko deserved another chance, too. Sliding next to him, she rested her cheek against his back. As she listened to his even breathing, her body eased and a sense of all-was-right-with-the-world seeped into her along with his warmth.

****

Fire raged in his belly, and he'd ground his teeth

together so hard his head ached. That damn bitch with her blasted luck. Well, it wouldn't last forever. He'd seen to that. There was one less man to protect her now.

And they thought they were so smart. He'd show them who was the smartest.

Laughing viciously, he rubbed his hands together. Hate had spread inside him like cancer, and he enjoyed the malignant thoughts that consumed him.

Almost time.

Soon, he'd have Janko out of the way, too.

Chapter Nine

The cell phone on the bedside table buzzed, then began to vibrate. Janko awoke with a jerk, snatching the offensive black machine before it landed on the floor. He shut off the alarm and rechecked the time on the display. "Damn! We slept the night away." The covers had tangled around his legs, entrapping him.

KC leaned over, her breasts pressed into his arm. "That's not all we did last night." Her voice, thick and sultry, held the promise of more passion.

"We ate a meal that didn't come out of a sack."

She cuffed him lightly on the shoulder. "Yeah, well one of us ate in the sack."

"You're bad." He kicked free of the covers, then swung his legs to the floor.

"And you love me for it."

He looked over his shoulder at her kneeling in the middle of the bed with the sheet wrapped around her. *You're absolutely right, I do love you.*

As tempting as it was to delay going out, he had to find Bo, the man who'd made the bullet that killed Patrick. Long ago he'd introduced himself to Janko as Bonneville Henderson—*Custom Ammunitioneer—Special Loads for Special Toads*. The man reminded Janko of a weasel, but as he'd found out, no one could build a better bullet than Bo.

In the shower, he thought about how wonderful last night had been. After a nice dinner, he'd hired a carriage to take them through the Quarter and Garden District.

Parts of the city had recovered from Hurricane Katrina, while others still looked as bad as the day it happened. New buildings and total destruction. Life and death. The world still revolved despite the pain and loss.

When they'd passed by Bo's house, the collection of kids' toys scattered about the yard had made him smile. Same as the last time he'd seen it. He'd been happy to see that Bo's shop had survived the storm and looters.

This morning he would wait for his old friend at his shop just off Canal. Janko finished his shower, picked up his shaving kit, then put it down when he saw how late it was getting. There wasn't enough time to shave and get to Bo's before he opened. And he *had* to see Bo. The little man knew where every bullet he sold went. Kept all his records in his pea-sized head.

She passed him on his way out of the bathroom. "Give me ten minutes and I'll be ready to go," she called out.

"I've got to do this one alone." He pulled on a pair of faded jeans and a loose fitting T-shirt.

"What?" She poked her head around the corner as he checked his weapon.

"I'll only be gone a short time, then we're outta here." He tucked the gun into the holster clipped inside his waistband, then used the shirt to conceal it. "Bring you back beignets."

Hurt registered on her face, but she shrugged a shoulder. "I want a big cup of coffee and the beignets better be hot." She disappeared into the bathroom, and as he locked the door, he could hear the water running.

The closer he got to Bo's unmarked shop, the more his gut clenched. Pros didn't leave casings at jobs. Certainly not casing with identifiable head stamps. Casings that contained custom ordered bullets.

Casings that provided evidence.

Stupid must be tattooed on his forehead. He'd fallen for one of the oldest tricks in the book. The shooter had left the brass on purpose, knowing he'd find it and come back here to Bo.

As he approached the shop, he drew his gun. He could see that the door hung at an angle. Slipping into the shadowed corner, he waited for his eyes to adjust and listened.

Nothing.

But he knew someone was watching him. He could feel the cold hate boring into him. The siren he heard in the distance came closer, then suddenly outside, tires squealed and car doors slammed. "Come out with your hands up."

A thin shaft of light appeared briefly in the back of the shop. Whoever been there had slipped away, but it was too late for him. He melted into the surroundings, becoming invisible as the police searched the shop. They found poor Bo, his throat slit ear to ear, his eyes frozen wide in fear, and an infinity mark carved on his forehead.

Sweat popped on Janko's brow and trepidation settled like a brick in his belly as he realized he'd been set up. He'd fallen into the trap no novice would have. Shit, how could he have been so stupid? Now he was pinned down here. There was no way to escape until after the police left. No way to warn KC. No way to protect her. She was alone and at the mercy of her pursuer.

****

"I'll be right back. Don't leave. I won't be gone long." KC sarcastically repeated Janko's words as she wore a path in the ugly shag carpet. Any noise—whether real or in her too vivid imagination—had her spying out the break in the curtain to see if it was him.

"Sure you won't be gone long," she mumbled while she walked from the window around the bed to the bathroom door. She'd passed edgy after Janko had been gone thirty minutes. Now, two hours later, she bordered on panic.

Where the hell was he? Making those beignets himself?

Or was he not telling her everything because he

didn't trust her? She picked at a nick in her thumbnail. The popping noise was only slightly less irritating than the cranky air conditioner.

"Be ready to go when I get back." Her tone grew more mocking. *I'll show you ready to go.* Right after she made certain he was all right, she planned to let him have it with both barrels for worrying her unnecessarily.

Pulling out the last of her clean clothes, she tossed his T-shirt on the floor, and quickly dressed. She stuffed her gear bag with her dirty clothes, tucked the locket back into the Bible before placing in the bag. Dammit, she'd even pack for him.

Retrieving his shaving kit from the bathroom, she realized he'd left in a hurry. He never went anywhere without shaving. She tugged firmly on the heavy zipper, but it hung on something inside. Moving to bedside table, she turned on the lamp with one hand as the other one dumped the contents of the kit on the bed.

The first thing she reached for was the tiny cell phone with the blinking red light. She sank on the bed, absently pushing the rest of the stuff aside. Feeling as dim as the 40-watt bulb next to her, she simply stared at phone for a minute.

Janko must have turned it on before he left so he could contact her, but had forgotten to give it to her. She flipped the cover up and saw she'd missed a call. Selecting the redial feature, she waited for him to answer and one handed scooped his belongings back into his kit.

The warbled tone that came on the line sent chills dancing up her spine. It'd been so long since she'd connected to an agency cut out phone. They weren't all that different from a PBX at a big company, except Pegasus' were traceless and portable. Just like answering voice mail on her cell phone, she tried to reassure herself, but her fingers trembled slightly as she entered her old PIN. She heard a few clicks, clinks and switches in the line before a mechanically altered voice answered.

Her shoulders sagged, then stiffened as the voice

said, "Intelligence report: Janko is in danger. Trap waiting. Find now before too late."

She sucked in a frightened breath. "Where? Where?" The silence of the dead line faded until replaced by the beating of her heart. *I've got to go to him.* She rushed out the door, but before it could close, she came back. Grabbing her bag, she shoved the clothes aside until she found her gun and slid it in her pocket.

Heat waves shimmered on the asphalt between the rows of parked cars. Old storied buildings crowded the narrow alley, towering above her like canyon walls. The air grew heavier and more fetid the closer she got to the river.

She couldn't jog fast enough, or get there quick enough, to outrun her fears that she'd be too late to save Janko. Her clothes, plastered to her wet body, bound her limbs, slowing her. She didn't even know where to start looking. Sweat rolled into her eyes, and she swiped at her brow and cheeks with the back of her hand. *I can't lose him now.*

In the few short days they'd been together, she'd come alive again. She remembered the things he'd done that made her smile. Made her laugh. Made her love him again. She could still feel the warmth of his hands as he became reacquainted with her body.

The old-fashioned three globe pawnshop sign reeled her attention back to the situation at hand. Would someone in there know about the ammunition maker? She had to try as she found the right door to enter and ambled to the glass display case that held the guns.

"You sell ammo with those guns?"

The clerk behind the counter glared at her. She waited for him to answer, but when he didn't respond, she pressed on. "You know anybody who makes bullets around here?"

"Lady, I don't know nobody who does nothing like that. Get out. I don't need no trouble."

She met with the same hostility in the second, third

and fourth shop. Clerks, and some of the customers, acted if she were on drugs, or worse, a fed. Yeah, she was an agent all right—an agent of death ready to kill for the man she loved. Her frustration rose with the temperature and each second that ticked by whittled away at her temper.

The long whistle blast from the Steamboat Natchez rattled nearby shop windows and made most tourists glance toward the docks. She was able to rapidly scan the knots of people. But no Janko. Her heart sank a little deeper. Another steamy whistle echoed through the Quarter as she sidestepped an obnoxious clown making balloon animals. His partner danced to the calliope music from the Natchez, then made rude comments to those who failed to add money to their gaudy tip bucket.

For a split second, she considered burying her gun in the clown's rainbow colored hair to see if he could pale whiter than his make-up. But someone would call the police and she didn't need that kind of involvement.

Or did she?

****

He sat on the patio of the Café Du Monde, sipping a *café au lait*. New Orleans wasn't a city that made his Top Ten list or even in the top twenty. He thought the river smelled, and the cuisine gave him gas. Why KC loved it so, he was clueless. The hurricane had done its best to wiped out the city, but it hadn't killed the spirit that still lived on. Even the tourists had started coming back, making the French Quarter seem crowded. Like now.

Big ones, little ones, old, young, black, white, and skin tones in between. Red heads, brunettes, raven, and blondes. A group of teens, clad in black trench coats, stomped by his table and he wrinkled his nose at their multiple piercing, psychedelically dyed hair fashioned into spikes, and the pervasive odor of dope that followed like the moth-eaten dog they dragged on a chain. He would make damn sure his daughter never looked, or acted, like that. And if she did, she'd be locked in her room without food or water until she saw the error of her ways.

Stationed on one of the crossroads of the Quarter, he had an open view to each new wave of tourists making their way down the street. All that was required of him was to bide his time. Just as he'd counted on, he saw KC racing down the street on her futile mission to save Janko. Foolish bitch had chosen Janko over him, and in doing so, had sealed hers and Janko's fate.

Almost time.

To watch them both die.

****

Janko obeyed every traffic law, observed every speed limit, did everything not to draw attention to himself as he made his way back to the motel. He burst through the door only to see the old woman from the office sitting on the bed, her dirty slippers on top of the bags.

"Don't think you can skip without paying another's day rent." She pointed a gnarled finger at him that he wanted to snap off. "It's after 12, and you won't get your luggage back either."

His anger erupted in a low feral growl. Digging into his pocket, he removed a wad of cash, then threw some bills at her. "The lady who was here, where is she?"

"Gone like a bat out of hell. Left you, huh? Not much of a lady, unless she was one of those 'evening' types." A curler flew across the room as she tossed her head back, howling with laughter.

Grabbing her by the throat, he hauled the old woman off the bed until her feet no longer touched the floor. "If she happens to return, tell her I'll be back. You can bet your life on that, and if anything happens to her while she's here, you can kiss your life goodbye."

Through blue-tinged lips, the old woman sucked in as much as her constricted throat allowed. Her eyes bulged in fear. But he wasn't finished with her yet. He gave her a rough shake to keep her attention focused. "Did you see which way she went?"

"Le-f-tt."

Janko released his grip and she slithered to the bed like limp spaghetti.

"You're crazy," she called out after him.

No doubt about it, he was crazy and he didn't care. He had to find KC. Nothing else mattered. Driving like a maniac, he navigated the streets and alleys looping the Quarter in an ever-tighter circle. He should have brought her with him this morning. Never should have left her alone.

He gave a cursory glance into every glass-fronted shop, trying to spot her. His attention zeroed in on a woman he thought was KC in line buying a ticket for the sternwheeler. He jammed on the brakes, the car skidding to a stop, then he abandoned it in the middle of the street. He raced toward the woman as she boarded the boat. Elbowing people out of the way, he leapt over the rope railing onto the gangplank, where an attendant asked for his ticket.

"I don't have one." Janko watched the woman go inside the vessel.

"Then you'll have to leave."

"This is an emergency. I have to get on." He dropped his gaze to the boy, who looked barely old enough to shave. His hands clenched into fists. Knock the kid out, or toss him into the water. Either one would be so easy.

"Uh-huh, sure, I get that all the time. Can't you think of a more original excuse?" The young man placed his fists on his hips, blocking Janko's way.

"I've got to get on that ship." He took a menacing step forward, then from his pocket, he flashed the boy two twenty-dollar bills. "Will that ticket do?"

"Welcome aboard the Natchez, mister. Enjoy your voyage." He quickly palmed the bills as he stepped aside.

Janko took the steep stairs two at a time to the first deck. He searched the dining area, the deck, the second level, then on third deck, he spotted her on the starboard side as she was pulling a chair to the railing.

He sprinted over, touching her on the shoulder. "KC."

The excitement that had been building inside him burst like a bubble when the woman turned.

She eyed him up and down, then back to rake his face with a smoldering gaze. "No, but I wish I was."

He murmured an apology, then left the boat as the anchor was rising. If he ever needed his sixth sense to kick in, he needed it right now.

"KC," he yelled. People stared at him. Several hurried away. A path cleared across the trolley tracks. He walked against the flow of the crowd to the curb and found his car hooked to the back of a tow truck.

"Wait!"

He ran after the slow-moving truck as far as Jackson Square. The light turned red and Janko walked to the driver's window. "Hey, mister—"

The blue barrel of a .45 caught him in the throat. The driver grunted, "I don't want no trouble, son. Ya hear?"

Janko raised both hands in mock surrender. "Sure thing," he said as he moved to the curb. The light changed to green, and he watched his rental stutter down the street. *Now what* mingled with the *What else can go wrong* despair centered inside him.

The last chime from the clock in the St. Louis Cathedral hung in the tepid air. Crossing the park, he stood in front of the church, looked at the rising spire, and he prayed for the first time since he was a boy. "God, help me." Neither knowledge nor relief came to him, but guilt did. And the pain was unbearable. He'd failed her, quite possibly for the last time.

Everyone he loved died.

****

Live oak trees along Decatur formed an arbor shading the crowded sidewalk, slightly cooling the air, but did nothing to cool KC down. The last time she'd been in New Orleans, mounted police had been on every corner. Now that she needed one, there were none to be found.

Up ahead, a gaggle of blue-haired old ladies effectively stopped foot traffic as they huddled around a street artist. When KC walked on the edge of the curb, two tour buses screeched to a stop beside her. The old women reminded her of a flock of chickens as they scattered to find their errant mates, then clucked admonitions as they quickly lined up to board. When the doors opened, the senior citizen mob surged forward, bumping and jostling her until she almost went down.

Fighting her way clear, she managed to step in between the buses when the lead bus took off. A cloud of diesel smoke muddied the air and the stench clung to her. Her eyes watered as the fumes filled her lungs. Halfway across the street, she thought she heard her name and spun about. The second bus zoomed by, narrowly missing her.

"Janko?" *I'll find him. I've got to find him.* She refused to give up hope. He'd stirred more than her blood, he'd reopened heart.

As she made her way up the sidewalk, she quizzed every vendor along the square if they knew the man who made the bullets. Stopping at the psychic in front of the cathedral, she asked the woman, who nodded then stuck out her hand to demand payment in advance. KC emptied her pockets, then begged for an answer, but the woman noisily shooed her away. KC's head drooped until her chin rested on her chest. Her shoulder nudged a person walking the other way. "Sorry," she said automatically without looking up.

"Kelly? Kelly Garretty?"

The voice sounded familiar. She came to a standstill, taking a long incredulous look. It couldn't be, could it? She'd already been wrong once today. "Art? What are you doing here?"

"Looking for you. Janko sent me to find you. I ran into him and he asked me to hunt for you."

"Janko." She spun three hundred and sixty degrees searching for him, excitement building like a thunderstorm inside her. "Where is he?"

"He's on his way and should be here shortly." His

eyes were shining brightly. His wide smile showed perfectly capped teeth, but she missed the hardness that flashed briefly across his face.

She gave him a quick hug. "It's so good to see you."

Taking a moment, he held her at arm's length, assessing her. "It's hard to believe, but I think you're even more beautiful than the last time I saw you, if such a thing is possible. Time has treated you well."

"You, too. I almost didn't recognize you wearing T-shirt and shorts instead of an Armani. And that ball cap! Makes you blend in with the rest of the bubbas."

"Gee, thanks, I think." His grin faded. "Let me bring you up to speed over a drink, then you *must* fill me in on what's happened all the years we've been apart." He rubbed his hand along her arm.

"Up to speed?" She looked at his hand and he removed it.

"Janko and I are partners. Have been since you left the agency."

"Oh?" She raised an eyebrow in concern.

"Don't look so surprised. There are a lot of things you don't know about him. Let's get that drink while we wait for Janko."

She was hot, tired, and worried, in addition to hurting inside. How could Janko have kept so many secrets from her? After the last few days, did he not trust her? Maybe she did need to sit and sort things out.

Her old friend motioned down Pirate's Alley, and she saw a couple of tables on the walkway, their red and white umbrellas fluttered invitingly in the small breeze. Something cool would relieve her parched throat, perhaps douse her burned spirit, too. As Sandusky escorted her to the café, she startled when his hand hovered at the small of her back. An unpleasant prickle crept up her spine. Upon entering, she would have stayed at the counter, but he shook his head.

"Why don't you find us a seat while I place our order. I think I see one that's under a fan."

Neon signs on the walls provided the scant light as she made her way to small table. *A boxcar has more room than this place.* Sitting with her back to the wall lessened her claustrophobia and allowed her to watch people go by as she waited.

Janko?

She jumped to her feet too fast and her chair banged against the bricks. When it bounced into her knee, she lost her footing, then landed hard on her bottom. Had she just seen Janko? No, if it'd really been him, he'd have come in. She was seeing things again. But... if it was him and he hadn't come in, she'd shoot him. Her hand pressed against her shorts for her gun, but it wasn't there. Using her foot, she tapped the floor around her, finding nothing. She took a fast peek under the table where she saw that the floor was layered with grime and old bits of food, but no gun. She heard approaching footsteps and straightened in time to see Sandusky hold up two tall curved glasses.

Art set down the frosty and fruit-topped concoctions. "I just couldn't resist getting Hurricanes. It's so touristy." He smiled as he slid the drink in front of her, then scooted his chair closer.

"You seem a bit distracted. Is everything all right?" Instead of looking at her, he examined the people passing by outside.

"Oh, sure," she lied. She wasn't sure about anything anymore, except for the uneasiness rising in her belly. Picking up her glass, she raised it. "To old friends and new beginnings."

Their glasses clinked with the toast and she took a small sip. She'd forgotten how syrupy sweet the drink was. Taking the straw, she blended the rum from the bottom with the fruit juices on top, and tasted it again. "It's good." She gave him a weak smile, then took a big gulp of the Hurricane.

"So, what have you been doing for all these years?" He leaned across the table, but quickly changed positions to admire the close-up view of the teenage waitress—

wearing cutoffs that were just this side of indecent—as she bent over to set a heaping mound of boiled crawfish and sauces on the table.

"I didn't know you liked crawfish." KC said the first thing that entered her mind, relieved to avoid his question for now. Grabbing a cold red crustacean, she cracked open the shell, took the tail out and dipped it into the bowl of cocktail sauce before popping it into her mouth. The crawfish, rubbery and off-flavor, had been steamed too long. She took a big gulp of her drink to wash away the taste.

"There's nothing like good food, good drink and good company." He peeled a couple, but left them on the plate as he scrutinized her.

Drawing a deep breath, she let it escape as a long exhausted sigh. Damn she was tired and her head pounded like an overworked bass drum. Rubbing her temples didn't ease the relentless beat. A cold thundering wave swept over her and with it panic as her vision began to fuzz. She knew she was exhausted, but didn't think the alcohol could have worked this quickly. The fogginess in her brain was similar to when she'd taken too much pain control medicine after becoming hurt last year.

Oh My God, she'd been drugged. Art had put something in her drink. Forcing her eyelids wider, she focused on him and his gaze ricocheted off hers. She gasped, her lungs on fire. The air around her seemed nonexistent, as if she were in a vacuum. Fighting the effects of the drugs, she struggled to stand, but her legs refused to obey.

From behind her, he grabbed her waist and hauled her into him. His fetid breath scorched her cheek. "Remind me to thank Janko the next time I see him."

"W-what?" The ringing in her ears caused his words to sound tinny.

"I'd like to thank him for bringing you to me in such fine shape because you're mine now. Time to go, love."

"N-no," she wheezed. Janko didn't—wouldn't—betray

her. Not after all they'd gone through.

When he pivoted her away from the chair, her hand swung in a wide arc, knocking her drink over. The tall glass broke, releasing the Hurricane to spread across the table like a red tide. Sandusky's face came at her as if she was looking at him through a convex lens with his nose too large and his eyes black and beady. The room began to spin. Lightheadedness contrasted with ice heavy limbs, her heart sledgehammered against her ribs. The contents of her stomach hung at the base of her throat.

With one hand in the middle of her back, and the other vise locked on her upper arm, he maneuvered her around the café tables and into the alley.

The foliage from the garden behind St. Louis Cathedral blurred green, and the brightly painted pastels of the houses ran together like a rainbow.

As he guided her down another street, she missed the curb and fell headfirst onto the sidewalk. With the wind knocked out of her lungs, she lay motionless for a few moments. Her breath returned in strangled puffs as she crawled to the side of a building. Pain knifed through her as she leaned against the cool brick. Something warm and wet trickled down her cheek. She swiped at it, and through the haze, she saw that her fingers were bloody. Her eyelids slammed together. Flashes of Osprey swirled around her like the changing colors and patterns in a kaleidoscope. Sagebrush stained with blood. Blue uniforms on ochre sand. The sun broke over the dark mountains.

An intense light burned into her brain. A wild fire within her veins melted the numbness in her body and left in its wake exposed nerve endings. The street noises intensified. Covering her ears, she couldn't block out the clamor and she teetered on the crest of a black wave. She opened her mouth but instead of a scream her body danced as if aluminum foil had be scrubbed against her teeth. Bile rose in her throat.

A chuff of warm air brushed her arm and she felt

beads of sweat dot her upper lip. She forced her eyelids up as wide as a slit. The hairy gray shape that finally morphed into the muzzle of a horse, then she focused on yellow stripe against black. A New Orleans police officer squatted beside her.

"Well, what do we have here?" He pushed his hat back, and for just a moment, she thought it was Janko. KC wanted it to be him as she stretched out a trembling hand, which Sandusky grabbed.

"Officer, she tripped and needed to rest a few minutes."

"That cut probably could use some stitches." He stood, adjusted his hat, then climbed on his horse, the leather creaking as he settled into the saddle. "And you'd better sober her up."

Don't go! her mind yelled. Don't leave me.

"Yes, I will. Our room is just across the street. Thank you, Officer, for your concern." Sandusky waited until the cop rode around the corner before jerking KC to her feet.

Art couldn't be the one after her. No. Not Art! She'd loved him like the brother she'd always wanted. But he was taking her away from Janko, and that wasn't right. She flailed at his chest. Her muscles were no more effective against him than if they'd been made of Jello.

He wrapped her against him, pinning her left arm and half-carrying her into the alley. Whispering in her ear, "You'll never get rid of me. At least, not until I have our daughter."

KC's thoughts swirled at tornadic rates. Our daughter? Ashley? Bullshit. You're not her father, you stupid fuck. You'll never get close 'cuz Janko has hidden my babies. Her anguish acted like a counteragent to the drug. The fogginess in her mind wasn't as acute.

He flung her against the back of a tall white vehicle and held her upright with his forearm as he fumbled in his pocket for the keys. "Climb inside like a nice little girl, and Daddy will give you a treat," he said with menacing sweetness as he opened one of the cargo doors.

Knowing it meant her death if she got into the van, she had to escape. But how? The drugs had left her limbs powerless to outrun him. Her mouth, dry as cotton, prevented her from screaming "fire." There was only one option available to her.

She went limp.

Chapter Ten

"You bitch!" Sandusky tried to catch her, but she slid from his grasp, collapsing in a heap on the asphalt. In frustration, he kicked her in the stomach and received some satisfaction from hearing her moan.

Oh, it would be so easy to kill her now. Just do her and leave her like the piece of garbage that she is. But then she wouldn't be able to see me take our precious daughter away. A grin pulled his lips into thin slashes as he opened the other panel door. He wanted her to suffer as he'd suffered for too many years without his *real* family.

Almost time.

His excitement rose like the bulge in his pants as he envisioned what he had planned for her. He was going to leave her alive a few more days. Let her watch him filet Janko one strip at a time, then he'd do things to her until she begged him to kill her.

He hauled her to her feet, ready to drop her in the back of the van, when she sank her teeth deep into his forearm. Out of instinct, he let her go, but she grabbed him. As he attempted to jerk free she used his momentum to topple them over. He landed with a grunt as the force of their combined weight ripped the air from his lungs. Still stunned, he missed catching her before she rolled under the van.

"You can't get away from me, KC. I'm *never* going to let you go. *Never.*"

The uneven bricks cut into his flesh as he crawled toward her. Swiping his hand under the vehicle, he looped the edge of her shirt with a finger, but couldn't hold her when she moved farther in.

Disgusted, he stood, then dusted the bits of debris from his clothing as he walked to the driver's door. Time had taught him patience, and time was on his side. It always had been. It always would be. He climbed inside the van and started the engine. If the fumes didn't get her, he knew it wouldn't be long until it got very warm under there. He'd simply run over her legs, then drag her out.

Adjusting the outside mirrors so he could watch if she came out on either side, he didn't have to wait long until he saw the tips of her tennis shoes showing. No, he wouldn't get out yet, but let her cool her heels, so to speak. He laughed at his own play on words. He was so damn smart, he even amazed himself.

A door in the alleyway opened, distracting him, as a young man with a dirty apron tied around his waist came out. Sandusky made eye contact with the guy, then slid his hand between the seats, bringing a gun across his chest.

"Hey, mister, you can't be parking in this alley. We gotsa de-liv-ery coming."

****

A single gunshot rang out, stopping Janko in midstride. Before the echo faded, a woman's scream replaced it.

"KC!" Cold froze his heart. He was too late. If she'd been killed... He wouldn't let himself think that way as he sprinted toward an overflow crowd that spilled from the alley entrance onto the sidewalks. A couple of carriages blocked traffic as passengers stood to get a better look. The drivers sawed on the reins, trying to keep their fidgety mules in place.

Janko dodged the nervous animals, then shoved people aside as he bullied his way to the front. There he saw KC clinging outside the driver's side window of a van, her shoeless feet dragging the pavement as the vehicle arced forward and back.

"Somebody help that woman."

"Watch out, he's trying to get away."

"She's going to be run over for sure."

The closer he got, he could see she'd gripped the steering wheel, her head tucked between her arms to protect it from the driver's pounding fist.

"You!" Janko wasn't sure if he'd spoken as his gaze zeroed in on Sandusky. Molten steel replaced icy fear. His hand itched. He'd never wanted to kill someone so badly.

The van pulled forward, forcing him to jump back. His foot struck something on the ground and he heard it clatter, but wouldn't take his eyes off KC. He knew he'd only have one chance to pull her free. He paused to get timing. As the van lurched, he sprang, tackling her around the waist.

"I've got you, babe. Let go." Her body melted into his and they landed with a thud, his arms still tight around her. Black tires bore down. At the last second, Janko spun them to safety. The swoosh of air on his back made him to flinch. A man from the crowd rushed in and grabbed KC.

The van's tires screeched, leaving black marks as it backed down the alley. Janko shook his head, trying to rid his nose of the stench of burning rubber. From his peripheral vision, he spotted the gun he must have kicked aside. In one smooth motion, he reached for the 9mm, brought it up, firing at the fleeing van. When a bullet struck the windshield, the vehicle sideswiped a Dumpster.

He got off two more shots, the plink of puncturing metal made him grin. But his half-smile sagged as the van whipped from the alley onto St. Anne, smoke rolling from the tires as it pealed out. Now standing in the middle of the street, he emptied the remainder of the clip into the retreating vehicle. With some satisfaction, he saw gasoline stream from the vehicle when it rounded the corner.

A hand clamped down on the gun, and he whirled around ready to nail the shit out of the intruder.

"You got some explainin' to do, boy."

He faced a burly cop, then saw a younger version separate KC from the crowd, then lead her up the ally. It was going to take a whole lot of fast-talking—if he was even believed—to hurry back on Sandusky's trail before it grew cold. He couldn't let the bastard get away, or she'd never be safe.

"Do you know this woman?" The cop jerked his head toward KC as she staggered up.

Janko looked at her and his heart ached for her. Blood and bits of garbage matted her hair. Her eye was swelling quickly and an ugly bruise had formed on the cheek below it. Her bottom lip was split. She held the tire marked and flattened sneakers in her scratched right hand, and the skin on her knees was like Shredded Wheat. He had to stop himself from taking her into his arms when she reached out toward him.

"Not before today, but I did see her with that man in the white van that sped away from here."

Her jaw dropped, and she fixed a pain-filled stare at him. He knew his denial had wounded her soul, but to reassure her now might mean he wouldn't catch Sandusky. And his first priority was to ensure her safety, no matter the cost to their relationship.

"Lady, do you have family or anyone we can call to meet us at the hospital?"

She shook her head. "No, not any more." Her words came out slurred but he understood her declaration. His betrayal knifed his heart.

Before he could signal her, an explosion ripped through the French Quarter, knocking them to their knees. Shards of glass from the windows above them rained down, and he covered his head and neck. As he slowly rose, he noticed the young cop had sheltered KC. Jealousy zinged through him. He knew *he* should have been the one holding her.

"What in tarnation was that?" the older cop asked as they all turned toward the black smoke billowing above the rooftops.

Janko suspected the gas from Sandusky's van had ignited, but he longed for a visual confirmation. He wrung his hands together and fidgeted until the older cop noticed.

"What's wrong with you?"

"This is frightening. I'd like to get out of here." He tightened his throat so his voice cracked as he spoke. "I was just trying to be a good Samaritan for this poor woman."

Two more explosions shook the ground.

"Damn." The cop looked at KC. "Ma'am, a car should be here real soon to take you to the Medical Center.

"That's not necessary. I'll be all right."

"At least let the paramedics look at those cuts." The young cop still had his arm around her.

"He's right," the older cop said before turning to his partner. "Make sure she's okay, then get her statement, and I'll finish up with this guy."

The wails of sirens filled the air and an ambulance arrived. KC leaned on the young cop as he helped to the back of the EMS truck.

Janko finished giving his statement and left, walking in the opposite direction of where he wanted to go.

Circling the police perimeter, he cut through alleyways and side streets. The blast had broken windows for at least two blocks. He followed the scattered glass as if it were breadcrumbs to a lump of twisted metal smoldering on a blackened pavement. He had no trouble blending into the background. The few police officers had their hands full trying to control the ever increasing and unruly onlookers. Another car fire kept the firemen busy.

Through the rising heat waves, Janko spied the distorted image of a rundown townhouse. Upon closer inspection, he noticed most of the paint had peeled, exposing old gray wood. Missing mortar made the bricks stand out like gaps between bad teeth. The ironwork had rusted, and the shutters that survived the blast hung odd angles next to nonexistent windows. A pigeon flew out, then veered to avoid the noise and heat.

He backtracked to the alley to find a high wall guarded the ancient building. Vines and Spanish moss draped from an overhanging tree and overgrown ivy had sent little brown fingers into the old brick. Concertina wire and broken bottles set in concrete lined the top. Visitors weren't welcome coming in from this direction.

Grabbing a handhold of greenery, he hoisted himself up, digging the toe of his shoe in the crumbling masonry. With his other hand, he stretched to grasp the lower limb. The unmistakable crack of wood made him cringe. His heart slammed against his chest while he centered his weight. The vines in his hand pulled away leaving him dangling by one arm. He stilled the sway of his body by hooking his foot through the ivy. The muscles under his arms and ribs burned at the strain of holding all his weight.

The branch drooped farther as he eased his other hand up, then sidled a few hand-slides closer to the tree trunk. His feet found a solid perch amid the denser parts of the vegetation and he slowly he pulled himself up until he could kneel on the wall. The glass had been broken out and the wire cut, telling him someone had used this way before. He dropped to the courtyard, his shoes crunching on leaves the wind had blown into thick piles as he walked to the back door. The doorknob turned easily in his hand.

Sounds of tiny feet scurrying preceded him as he made his way through the empty house. He loped up the stairs to the second floor to a partially covered front window. From his vantage point, he watched the investigation. He wanted to see Sandusky's body, or the parts that were left, before he'd be satisfied the man was really dead. Until then, he would wait.

An hour had elapsed by the time he saw KC again. A female officer had brought her to the scene. She'd been cleaned up, her forehead and hands were bandaged. As she surveyed the destruction, she looked directly at him. Instinctually, he ducked even though he knew she couldn't see him behind the shutter. When they'd been a team, they could feel the other's presence. Did she still have that ability? Maybe she was expecting him to be here. She would if it were him down there.

The officer spoke to her and she turned to view a sheet-covered body. When the sheet was pulled back, he saw her nod, then point at the arm. After she spoke to the investigator, he removed the watch, then flipped it over.

Of course, he'd forgotten that she'd given Sandusky a Rolex for his birthday one year. Art had been in such a black mood that she thought a surprise birthday party would cheer him up and had hidden the watch inside the cake. That had been right before they'd shipped out for Osprey.

Osprey, the beginning of all their troubles, the end of their relationship. He lived with the choice he'd made everyday of his life, and hated it. Sending her away was for the best. If he'd told her how much he loved her, she would have been taken from him too—just like everyone else in his life that he'd ever loved. There was no way he could survive if he'd have seen her in a coffin.

Life was cruel.

He wanted to love, wanted to fill the void, wanted those people who'd been ripped away from him returned. If only he could travel back in time, he'd change so many things starting with his grandfather. He saw the old man's face in the darkness, and he tried to stop the flood of memories.

He failed.

Janko had been the star pitcher for the ten and under little league team, and the regional playoffs were in Caddo Parish. He'd begged and pleaded with *Grandpere* not to work that day.

"You have to come to my game. We've never lost when you've been there. It's the playoffs. I'll never ask you for another thing," he whined as his grandfather finished strapping on the Sam Brown belt that held his holster, handcuffs, and ammunition.

"I'll be there, Cooter." He tousled the boy's hair. "That's a promise."

"Thanks, *Grandpere*." Giving his grandfather a big bear hug, he walked with him to the cruiser. He remembered how strong the old man's hands were on his scrawny shoulders. With his fingers gripping the wide leather belt, he gazed into his hero's face. "Don't forget, be there by 1:30, 'kay?"

His grandfather opened the car door, then leaned across it to look him in the eye. "I love you, boy."

"I love you too, *Grandpere*."

And with those words, Janko had killed his beloved grandfather. On his way to the game, Sheriff Claude Broussard took the back roads to save time through Caddo Parish and was ambushed during a traffic stop by three escaped convicts.

If Janko hadn't loved his grandfather so much and begged him to come, then *Grandpere* would never been on that road. He wouldn't have been rushing back to watch him play ball. He wouldn't have died.

A tear slipped, and Janko brushed it away. If he'd told KC from the start why he couldn't love her, she'd have believed him then. But not now.

It was too late to take things back. Too late to...

The tiny hairs on his neck rose and his senses went on alert. While thinking about the past, he'd let his guard down and was no longer alone in the room. The air swirled around him just before the blow struck his head.

****

An old-fashioned gas lamp glowed outside the shuttered window, illuminating the middle of the room. KC sat with her back against the wall, watching a cockroach scurry across the strips of light and shadow on the dusty wood floor. That's the way she'd kept her life since Osprey, afraid of exposure and racing for cover. Oklahoma had given her seclusion, marriage, a name change, and most important, safety. How naïve—no *stupid*—she'd been thinking her past would remain buried. Her false sense of security had put her children, and so many others, in danger.

Drawing her wounded knees to her chest, she rested her head on them, then let out a ragged sigh. She hurt. And it wasn't all from the fight with Sandusky. Her arms, her heart, her very soul ached. She wanted her children back. The extreme fear of never seeing them again had sped up her body's metabolism of the drug Sandusky had slipped her. Now, would Janko keep his promise to return them?

The roach had started up Janko's shirt, then backed down, altering its trek. She really should make sure he was still alive. He hadn't moved since she'd cold-cocked him seconds, or was it minutes, ago? Time had become so warped. Along with everything else in her life. Looking at her watch, she saw it'd been a while.

"Wake up," she called from across the room. No response came from him, not even when the roach neared his face. Would serve him right if it crawled all over him. After all, they were kin.

She started to get up and her groan resonated through the empty room. Stiff, sore muscles protested more exertion. She felt as if she'd been run over by a truck. Close. Strafed by a van. Taking a deep breath, she slowly straightened, then had to wait for the dizziness to subside. As she walked toward him, she kept in the shadows.

A twinge of guilt swept through her as she stood over his inert body. Guess she shouldn't have hit him that hard, but damn him, he'd betrayed her once more. Sold her out to Sandusky. Had lied to her over and over. Made her love him again.

And that may have been the biggest mistake of her life.

"Wake up." She nudged him with her shoe, then slammed her heel down. Pop-crack. Antennas, separated from the roach, wriggled while she ground the rest of the bug until only a wet spot remained on the floor.

"Janko, get up now, or I'll—I'll..."

A low grumble came from the prone man. "KC?"

She saw one eye open, then close, and when he tried to move, both eyes opened wide with surprise.

"What the hell?" He lay on his stomach, his arms and legs trussed together like a Thanksgiving turkey. His muscles bunched, then swelled as far as the restraints would allow. She backed up a few steps just in case the old electrical cord broke.

Watching him struggle made her laugh. "The more you move, the tighter it becomes.

"I see you're clearly enjoying this."

"Yes, I am. Call it a little bit of payback." She stood over him, controlling her impulse to give him a swift kick in the groin.

"Enough fooling around. Let me go." The amusement had left his voice.

"No."

"Why?"

"How dare you pretend." Like gasoline on water, her anger floated on the surface of her soul-aching hurt. One little spark could set her off. "Why? What did I ever do to you—other than love you—to make you betray me?"

"I don't know what you're talking about." He raised an eyebrow.

"Don't play your silly games with me. You and Sandusky. Partners from the get-go. You pigs planned all this."

"Sandusky?" Struggling against the cords, he succeeded in making them tighter. "I've never been partners with anyone but you." He gave her a derisive snort, then a head nod. "You've been sandbagged. He really got you good. Try to be logical and think this through. You're going to believe the man who tried to kill you instead of the man who saved you and your kids?"

"You guys are not the first to play Good Cop-Bad

Cop."

"Not my style, darlin'. I think the drugs fried your circuits. You're not thinking straight."

"Well, I don't know what, or who, to believe. Lies flow from your mouth like sweet promises." Disbelief welled inside her, along with the threat of tears. "Actions speak louder than words, Janko, but both hurt like hell when used against you. I can't trust you anymore."

He did the last thing she expected him to do. He laughed. Body shaking, deep-from-the-gut kind of laughter until his tears formed in the corners of his eyes.

"Oh, KC, that's rich." He closed his eyes, put his head on the floor, and relaxed so that only the cords remained taut.

"I had to have a little insurance that you'd tell me where my children are."

Time, measured by the steady beat of her heart, ticked by. He was quiet so long, she thought he'd fallen asleep. Inching a little closer to him, she remained wary and stayed out of his reach, just in case he'd slipped his bonds.

He spoke without looking at her. "Even if I gave you directions, I doubt you could find their location. And if you did stumble across it, without me, I doubt you'd get a glimpse of them, much less get them back."

She sank to the floor next to him, her shoulders sagging as defeat settled like a wet wool mantle. "You heartless prick. What would have happened if you'd been killed?"

"But I didn't get killed." He paused, then slowly opened his eyes. Their gazes collided, and his showed no compassion.

"To get your children back, you'll have to trust *me*. That's my insurance policy to keep you from killing me."

Frustration fueled her ire. She didn't want to trust him anymore, but she ruefully admitted that he was right. *Damn, I hate it when he's right and I hate it even more when I can't do anything about it.*

He patiently waited for her to undo the cords biding him and when he was released, his arms and legs hit the floor like over stretched rubber bands. She stepped back while he gathered himself together, arching his back, cat-like to stretch knotted muscles, then rub his limbs, which had to be prickling. "Damn, you did a good job, but I expect no less. Anything you do, you do well."

"You bet." Tapping her foot, she loomed over him, hands fisted on her hips. "Let's go. I want to be with my kids tonight."

Can't," he said as he began to straighten.

"What do you mean 'can't?'" She jerked him the rest of the way to his feet, her fingers tightly grasping his shirt. The thin fabric did nothing to stop the warmth of his skin from soaking into her hands.

She pursed her lips into a thin line, and he leaned forward ever so slightly. Was he going to kiss her? She should knock his block off. Or at least, pitch him to the floor. Instead, she pulled him into her, enjoying his sudden gasp. She'd really caught him off guard.

With every breath, she feathered his cheek, and made sure her breasts stroked his chest. As her nipples hardened, so did he. His arms tightened as if to cradle her against him, but she gently kneed his legs apart, her hip finding his pulsing erection. Sliding her leg up and down his inner thigh, she intensified the heat created by the rasping materials to set her blood on fire. She ran her tongue up the line of his jaw until she reached his ear. "Tell me 'can't' again, I'll make you beg for mercy."

Chapter Eleven

KC's heart pounded hard in her throat. In just a few minutes, she'd be holding her children. She'd never been separated more than a night from Ashley and Tyler, and this time—this time away—had irrevocably changed her life. And theirs.

As Janko's car sped down the deserted highway, she forced herself to stare at the white lines. Each one seemed farther apart than the last, like some ironic twist from a *Twilight Zone* show where the road stretched endlessly and the traveler would never arrive. Would she never get there? She'd quit asking him how much longer, afraid he'd say ten more minutes, or nothing at all.

The night yielded neither to the moon, nor the dawn. She noticed that it was just as dark here as it had been when they were airborne. In less than three hours, she'd gone from the French Quarter to a small airport, and by the time they'd cleared security, Janko's private jet had arrived.

After boarding, he'd gone to the back of the plane, whipping the dividing curtain closed. She'd tried to tell herself that the separation was what she wanted because she had ever right to be angry. He'd lied to her. He'd set her up as bait. He'd victimized her heart. And she hurt like hell at a time when she—they—should be celebrating the end of a successful mission. They should be in each other's arms.

She wandered to the front of the plane, rapped on the cockpit door, then opened it to find a wisp of a girl, who couldn't have been much older than Ashley, in front of the controls. "Hey, mind if I join you?"

The girl gave KC a brief glance before patting the seat beside her. "Not at all, I'd enjoy the company. You must be KC. Even if I hadn't seen you with Cooter—you call him Janko, right?—I'd have recognized you from seeing Ashley and Tyler. You have beautiful children."

"You know my kids? H—How? Are they all right? Do you know where they are?" A tightness clutched her chest as fought back emotions that would dissolve her control. She moved into the empty seat, buckled in, then stared at the girl. "Please—tell me?"

"Last Monday, I get a call to meet Cooter outside of some small town in Oklahoma no later than noon for a pick-up and delivery."

"He gave my kids to you?" KC lost her breath.

"Hey, what's wrong with that? I'm good with kids." The girl tried to act wounded, but the smile that lifted the corners of her mouth gave her away. "I usually never know what my cousin, or brothers for that matter, get me into. By the way, I'm Flavia, Evangeline's youngest, and only daughter. I run the family's charter service."

"What about my kids?" KC paused for a moment to settle her jumbled thoughts. "Were they terribly scared?"

"No, not too much—hesitant, wary. Once I talked to them, they were fine. Good kids."

The glow from the instrument panel highlighted the pixyish qualities of pilot's face. She had a sprinkle of freckles across her small nose, a mischievous twinkle in her eyes, high cheekbones, and lips that naturally curved into a smile.

As KC continued to scrutinize her, the young woman cocked her eyebrow. KC laughed. "You do that thing with your eyebrow just like Janko."

The young woman tilted back, her hair whipping around the seat, and snorted most unladylike. "Darlin', it's a Broussard trait." And then, she sobered. "Did I pass?"

KC's cheeks flamed. She was glad the dim light hid the evidence of her chagrin. "Sorry. I didn't mean to be rude, but the answer is yes." And she meant it. She liked this young girl, and something about her made KC realize that Janko had made sure her children had gotten the very best care.

"He did." Flavia stared straight ahead.

"What?"

"Made sure they had the best."

Had KC spoken? "Mind reader?"

"Something like that. I draw the line at family. Saints spare me! Who wants to know everything?" The girl laughed but KC detected a hint of sadness.

She changed the subject. "I noticed you call Janko, Cooter? How did he get a name like that?"

"Cooter is a baby turtle. Our grandfather called him that right after he was born. Guess he looked like one."

"Nicknames can be hard to escape."

"Well, you've got to admit, sometimes he acts like one."

Yeah, KC thought, he does.

The change in road noise brought her back to the present. Janko had turned on to a luminescent path, not much wider than the car. A house came into sight as the car rounded the last curve in the driveway.

Before the vehicle had come to a complete stop, she was bounding up the steps.

"Wait for me," Janko called after her.

But she couldn't wait as she tried the brass door handle, then shoved against the giant wood door with her shoulder.

"You're not getting in until..."

The door swung wide and KC barreled past a gray-haired woman who held it open. Dashing up the stairs to the first landing, KC turned. "Where are they?" Her voice sounded scratchy to her own ears. She glanced briefly at Janko and saw him slip his arm around the woman.

"Take a right at the hallway, third door on the left."

Racing up the steps two at a time, she reached the top and didn't slow until she'd opened the door.

Tyler, his mop of blond hair covering his face, looked so young, so angelic, that it took her breath away. She stifled a sob as she sat on the bed. Reaching out, she brushed his hair back, then placed a kiss on his forehead.

"Tyler? Slick? It's Mommy."

His eyelids fluttered, then he mumbled a sleepy, "Hi, Mom," before he turned onto his side.

She smiled wearily as she adjusted the covers. Pushing herself onto unsteady legs, she backed out of the room, afraid if she turned around, Tyler would disappear. But, that was nonsense she knew, because this was no dream and she'd be here in the morning when he awoke.

Once in the hallway, she saw Janko leaning against a doorjamb. He indicated with his head which door she wanted.

With a few steps she was in Ashley's room. The bed creaked as she sat. "Ashley, it's Mom." KC's hand trembled as she let her fingers trail against Ashley's cheek.

A nightlight from the hallway bathed the room with a golden glow, and she watched as long dark lashes parted to reveal vibrant blue eyes whose gaze focused quickly with recognition.

"Mom! Oh, God, it's really you." The girl sat up, then flung her arms wide, embracing KC. "You're home. I was so scared."

Me, too. She wanted to cry out as she buried her head in her daughter's auburn hair and hugged her tighter. "I'm here and I'm not leaving. Go back to sleep. We'll talk in the morning."

She pulled back, wiped Ashley's tears away as the girl lay down, then tucked in the quilts.

"Stay with me until I fall asleep, please, Mom?" A hand with glittery pink fingernails tugged on her arm.

"There's no place I'd rather be," she said as she rested against the headboard. Feeling her daughter nestle into her, she lightly stroked Ashley's head, humming an old lullaby like she'd done so many times, so long ago. Where had all the tomorrows gone? They'd become todays, which had turned into yesterdays, and piled into years. Seasons changed and her children had grown too fast.

She held her daughter, inhaling the herbal scent from the only shampoo Ashley used, and wondered how her daughter had convinced Janko, or that woman, to get that for her. Had it been a bribe for good behavior, or to keep her placated?

A breeze floated in from the partially opened window, and her daughter snuggled closer. KC closed her eyes, attempting to relax by matching Ashley's rhythmic breathing. As tired as she was, she had too much on her mind. Recrimination, self-doubt, and guilt weighed heavily on her. She'd let her children down, and hadn't kept them safe. They didn't even have a home to return to. There was so much to explain to them that she didn't know what to say or where to start.

And Janko? What about him? Where did she begin, or end, with him?

When the truth came out, and she had no illusions that she could hide the truth, would her children forgive her? Would she be able to forgive herself? She tipped her head back, resting the nape of her neck on a curl of the iron headboard.

"You can't be comfortable like that." Janko's hand, warm and heavy on her shoulder, brought her an odd sense of comfort, as if that simple touch reduced the overload of emotion coursing through her.

She opened her eyes just in time to see a smile fade away. "Can't sleep either?"

"No point now. It's almost dawn." He withdrew his hand, and with it, the brief emotional connection she'd had.

She shifted Ashley aside so she could get up without disturbing her. "I'd like to get cleaned up before the kids wake, but my clothes are missing. That's just fine with me, but I would have liked to get my mother's Bible and a few other personal things." She said this softly, more as a wish than a request.

He walked to the door, turned as if to say something. In the faint light, she saw a flash of sorrow in his eyes before he walled in his emotions. "I'll take care of it. Use the room at the end of the hall. Aunt E will set something out for you."

That being said, he left. The sound of his footsteps faded as he went down the stairs. Despite everything she'd promised herself after his betrayal fifteen years ago, despite the fact she'd told herself she was better off without him, despite her better judgment, she'd fallen in love with him anyway. Even as angry as she was at him for hurting her, she owed him for saving her children. As much as she loved him, she knew he could never love her. To protect what was left of her heart, she had to be sure not to confuse gratitude with love.

Looking out the window, she saw a slight gray line on the horizon. Yes, the sun was going to rise, and the world would keep turning no matter what her situation was. The bleakness of this moment would pass, and soon she'd get her life on an even keel.

One step at a time.

One day at a time.

She would get through this like she had before.

Alone.

****

Janko listened until the shower's glass door clinked shut before he entered his bedroom. Walking to the closet, he opened it and selected a few clothes from the armoire. As he stood there, he envisioned KC in the shower with the water raining over her. He longed to take the soapy cloth from her, slide it down her arms, across her breasts, belly and her long legs. His body reacted, making him uncomfortable. She'd broken the shell around his heart and had him on the edge of sanity. He hated himself for his weakness. He despised her for the power she held over him.

Maybe if he'd been honest with her, telling her why loving her could destroy him, then things would have been different.

But, he hadn't. He'd run away. Separated himself physically all those years ago, and again today—yesterday—on the jet. His need for solitude had brought him no answers, and had succeeded in pushing her away from him at a time when they so desperately needed to talk. What a fool he was.

The water stopped and he remembered the clothes he held. After laying them on the bed, he gave the bathroom door one last long look, then left.

****

Drying her hair with a towel, KC stepped from the bathroom into the bedroom. The wood floor was warm from the early morning sun streaming through the casement windows. As she slung the towel around her neck, she examined the room more closely. It was light and airy due to all the windows, and the French doors on each end opened onto shaded balconies. She could just imagine watching a storm as it passed. Each side would give her a commanding view of nature's fury. Or during the day to be able to follow the sun's progression as it marched across the sky.

But what caught her attention most was what the room didn't have. There were no curtains framing the windows, no rugs to soften the hardwood floor, and no furniture except a bed and nightstand. No pictures hung on the light blue walls, no photographs on the mantel; in fact there was nothing that would indicate someone actually inhabited the room. Only the large fireplace radiated comfort and warmth, even unlit.

Taking a few more steps, she rested her hands on a massive footboard. There on the bed was a pair of gray sweat pants and a faded burnt orange T-shirt. The clothes would do for the moment. She dropped the towel as she reached for the shirt. The white lettering, some peeling and others mere outlines, read "Property of the University of Texas Lady Longhorns."

She shook her head. After all these years, Janko had kept the shirt she'd given him. Soft and well worn—an implied statement about her—or was he trying to let her know he'd been telling the truth earlier? Maybe he'd never forgotten her. Maybe these were the first clothes his aunt selected for her. Maybe she was thinking too much. She shouldn't care that he'd kept a stupid old shirt. She shouldn't care about implied meanings.

And she for damn sure shouldn't care about him.

But she did.

She slipped the shirt on, smelling his scent that somehow still lingered. The soft fabric floated down her body as if it were a lover's light caress. Her heart beat faster as her mind succumbed to old memories. Heat flushed her skin. She could almost feel him behind her, his hands skimming across her hips, then slowly running under the shirt to tease her breasts. Her nipples hardened now as they did then. His easy touches had made her weak with desire and her body began to throb. His simple whispers had made her mind weak.

She'd loved him before, and he'd betrayed her. She'd trusted him before, and he'd broken that trust. Now he'd asked her to trust him again. Logic screamed 'No, no,' but her heart whispered 'Yes.'

Once upon time, she'd believed him, in a future with him. Now it was gone. The French door blew open, the breeze lifted a damp lock of hair from her face, sending a chill over her. A drop of water found its way down her back and she shivered, then wrapped her arms around herself.

Was love enough?

It hadn't been last time.

And this time, she was more scared than before. No longer could she make decisions based solely on her wishes. She was so damn afraid of making another mistake and screwing up her children's lives. Yanking on the sweats, she loosely tied them so they hung low on her hips. She picked up the towel, placed it on the rod in the bathroom, then padded barefoot down the stairs.

The smell of chicory led her into the kitchen where the older woman she'd seen when she arrived was sitting on a barstool, stroking a sleepy kitten in her lap.

"Mug by the pot is for you, *cher*. I'm Steven's aunt, Evangeline. You may call me Aunt E if you so wish."

KC returned the woman's intense gaze. "Thank you, Aunt E, for the coffee. It's so early, I didn't expect anyone to be up yet." Pouring herself a cup, she motioned with the coffee pot, then refilled the other woman's mug before replacing the pot back on the warmer. "I met your daughter last night."

"Ah, Flavia. I thought you might've."

"I'm KC, but I guess you already knew that." She sipped her coffee as a way of buying a moment to decide what to say. "I hope my kids weren't too much trouble. Sometimes they can be a handful."

"Children who were raised right are no trouble."

What in the world was that supposed to mean? "Well," she paused, "thanks for taking care of them." She pulled on one leg of the sweats. "And thanks for finding me something to wear. They're perfect."

A slow smile crossed Aunt E's mouth before she spoke. "I didn't, Steven did. He took care of you, 'cause I have no idea where that boy keeps his clothes. That's his room now and I haven't set a toe in there since my sister's died."

KC peered over the mug rim at her. Why tell her that? She didn't have long to contemplate any deeper meanings as the sound of a bark and what seemed to be a herd of horses galloping closer made her smile. She put down her coffee just in time for Tyler, followed by one of the biggest dogs she'd ever seen, barge through the swinging door.

"Aunt E! Aunt E, I dreamed—Mom! I didn't dream you. You're here, you're really here." He catapulted across the kitchen into her arms with the dog right behind.

"Hey, Slick." She drew him in close, planting kisses in his cottony hair until her throat painfully closed. Tears burned her eyes as she choked out, "I've missed you so much."

"Me, too, Mom, but you're squishing me."

He wriggled out of her grasp far sooner than she wanted to let him go, but then, she could have held him forever.

"Does Ashley know? Can I wake her up? Huh? Puh-leeze?" A mischievous glint danced in his eyes.

"Yes, no, and you'd better not. Remember how grouchy she is in the morning. She'll be down soon." KC ruffled his hair just before he turned to Aunt E.

"May I make breakfast?"

"Oh, *oui, m'ptit*." She brushed the cat from her lap and walked with Tyler into the pantry. "Let's see what we can find."

As Tyler put the last pancake on the wobbly stack, Janko and Ashley entered the kitchen from opposite directions. KC detected the immediate tension between them, and her heart sank. The wisp of hope that the people who meant so much to her could at least be nice to each other dissolved in the chilly air.

"Steven, are you going to join us?" Aunt E swept her arm toward the small table, set for five, as her dark gaze riveted on him.

"Yeah, I made enough." Tyler balanced the precarious hotcakes in one hand while holding the bottle of syrup in the other. "That way you'll be ready to take me fishin' on the bayou. Remember? You promised that when you got back, you'd take me where you used to go as a boy."

KC envied the faith and excitement she saw in her son's eyes, and cringed as she waited for Janko to tell him no. Janko didn't like to be told what to do. Janko didn't like kids.

Janko didn't like her.

So when he took the platter out of Tyler's hands and put it on the table, then smoothed down her son's ruffled hair, she was shocked.

"I'm going to pass on breakfast." He looked at her. *Trust me*, she read in his eyes. He returned his attention back to Tyler. "And if it's okay with your mom, we'll see what trouble we can find on the bayou."

"Can I, Mom? Puh-leez?" Tyler had scooted until his back pressed against Janko's legs. Janko laid his hand on her son's shoulder, then the two exchanged conspiratorial glances.

Her mouth fell open in disbelief. This situation was totally absurd. The old Janko she'd known would never do this, yet he acted like he actually wanted to be with Ty. Had she fallen into a parallel universe? Had aliens abducted Janko? He couldn't really be serious, could he? She allowed her gaze to drift between the two.

"Sorry guys, I'm not ready to let Tyler out of my sight just yet. Sorry, Slick, I've missed you too much." She tried for a winning smile.

"Oh Mom!"

"That's just great. He invites *Tyler* to leave this prison, but not me?" Ashley piped up angrily. Everyone turned toward her.

KC caught the jealousy in her daughter's voice.

"It's not fair, Mom. I really wanted to go. Me 'n Ash have been good. Please?" Tyler's soft brown eyes had grown puppy-like and pleading, making her feel guilty.

"I've been bored into insanity stuck here—no offense Aunt E—forced to wear the same thing every day since we got here." Ashley stuck both fists on her hips, then took a deep breath. "And if we can't go home now, I'd really like to get out even if it's for a little while. Mom—"

Before she could speak another word, Janko signaled stop with his hand. "Please, KC? I'd really like to show Tyler the bayou, and I had promised."

"Hey, mister, thanks a lot for noticing that I'm alive, too." Ashley gave him a go-to-hell-look.

"Watch it, young lady! You know better than that." KC cringed at her daughter's behavior no matter what the circumstances. "I'm sorry, Steven."

He flashed her a crooked smile. "Don't get mad at her. She's right. But, I propose a compromise. After breakfast why don't you ladies go shopping while us boys—" he winked at Tyler, "— go fishing. My treat." Up went that damn eyebrow.

Ashley's eyes widened in surprised, Aunt E smiled in a sly cat-like sort of way, and KC stood rooted to the floor, speechless, again not believing what she was witnessing. What was going on with Janko? Maybe aliens *had* sent a clone. With three, four counting Aunt E, against one, KC knew she was beaten. "I give. You guys win."

"Wooo-hoooo," whooped Tyler as he gave Janko a high five hand slap.

"Thanks." Ashley tossed her hair as she pulled out a chair, then plopped in it. "Be sure you leave plenty of money."

The corners of Janko's mouth lifted slightly. He draped his arm across Tyler's chest, pulling him in closer, then bent lower. "Hey, Slick, I'm outta here to get the boat ready. Come down to the dock when you're finished with breakfast." He stood, dropped some bills on the table, then gave a little bow as he mockingly tipped a non-existent hat, "Ladies, have fun."

KC sat on a stool, wondering what had just happened, and why she'd agreed to let Janko take her son for the day. Her thoughts skewed. Did he have another agenda? What if he used Tyler as a way to force her on another mission?

Or as a way to get even?

She took a sip of her coffee as the resolution came to her.

She'd kill him.

Chapter Twelve

After breakfast had been cleaned up and the dishes loaded into the dishwasher, Aunt E tossed KC her car keys. Then the three of them walked to the car parked in the circle drive.

"You sit with your mother. How can I back-seat drive from the front?" She climbed in, waving off the girl's attempt to help her into the car. "I may be a bit older than you, *cherie*, but I'm not dead."

The small town of Tulume looked like any other small town and could have belonged in any other state. In the center of downtown was a square with a white covered bandstand in the middle, and an aged statue of a horse and rider commemorating some local hero. The old buildings that lined the four intersecting streets had seen better days, as had the men who congregated on the sidewalk benches.

KC parked the car in front of Trudy's Best Dressed Shop, thought briefly of nice stores in Treaty Hill, then opened the car door.

"I'm going to run to the market while you girls shop." Aunt E looked at her watch. "There's a great café across and down the street. Let's meet for lunch at one. Will that give you enough time?"

KC looked at Ashley sitting on the car fender with the "whatever" attitude. Her daughter had been unusually silent during the drive. "Yes, it's a plan."

"*Cherie*, be sure you check out THE CADEAU." Aunt E was rewarded with a small grin from Ashley.

Teenagers! KC thought as she walked into Trudy's, not waiting to see if her daughter followed. As she made her way into the dress shop, the clerk greeted her with a cheery, "Hi, hon." Shortly, the bell over the door announced another shopper and the clerk sang out the same welcome.

The shop was far more impressive on the inside, with oak wall racks, spring fashions displayed against wallpaper that complimented instead of clashed, and dressing rooms with white saloon-type doors with stenciled flowering vines that followed the bowed shape. The thick carpet was comfortable under her feet as she easily went from rack to rack. There was a little bit of everything, designer labels, coordinates, casual dresses, T-shirts and shorts. She should have no trouble finding something to wear, but a restlessness nagged at her.

Stopping, she fingered a silk top. She took it from the rack, and the luxuriant fabric spilled over her hand like cool water. Refreshing, light, vibrant. This is what she needed in her life, her heart, her mind.

Ashley had made her way over and stood behind her.

"Mother, what happened? Why did you send that man to take us away? We could have stayed with Grandma Dorie, or even with Randy?"

KC put the shirt back.

"Mom?"

She turned, searching the young girl's troubled face and wanted to wipe the worry away, but she couldn't, no matter how hard she wished. Or what words she used.

"You're hurt." Ashley extended her hand. "Did *he* do that?"

KC stopped her from touching her face. "No, he didn't. Janko saved my life, and yours, and Tyler's. There's so much to explain, but I can't right now." *Because I haven't figured it all out.* "One day I'll tell you everything, I promise. Now, let's see if we can find some clothes." Giving her a quick squeeze, she was surprised when Ashley hugged her back and didn't let go first.

After locking the necessities, and a few outfits for KC in the car trunk, they still had time to check out the store Aunt E had suggested. Mother and daughter sauntered arm in arm across the street. But KC had the niggling feeling they were under surveillance. She sent Ashley on while she scrutinized the area. Nothing appeared out of place. The earlier crowd had dwindled to two old men sitting on the bench. One was whittling on a stick, stopping only to spit tobacco into a dirty Styrofoam cup, and the other used his hat to shoo flies. He waved at her. She waved back, then chided herself for acting so jumpy as she caught up with her daughter.

THE CADEAU instantly reminded KC of the late '60's with incense cloying the air, beaded curtains dangling across the doors, psychedelic posters on the walls that pulsed under black lights, mismatched shelves overflowing with a mixture of retro, eclectic, and the down-right strange. An older woman, who introduced herself as Sunshine, had long stringy brown hair, a leather headband across her brow, a batik halter-top and wide bell-bottom jeans with frayed hems. She flitted like a butterfly here and there with arms, hair and body waving as she showed Ashley around.

"Tight," "Sweet," "Right on," and a chorus of giggles floated to where KC stood, trying to decide if Tyler would like a small alligator head. Upon further and much clearer thought, she really wouldn't want him to have one. Knowing her son, he would stash it in some place where she'd least expect to see a reptilian head, scaring her half to death. She wandered through a maze of shelves, wondering if she'd ever find her daughter.

Ashley emerged from behind a sheet that covered a thumbnail of a dressing room, wearing an outfit that would send the fashion police in for an immediate arrest. "Isn't it cool, Mom?"

KC smiled weakly, then declined comment. The next sets of clothes Ashley modeled were all acceptable, even cute. In the end, her daughter's good taste prevailed. KC was as happy as the broad smile, and the new clothes, Ashley now wore.

The walk to the café took just minutes, and they hurried to where Aunt E stood waiting. Ashley held the door while KC and Aunt E entered first.

The three ladies made their way toward a booth in the back, when Aunt E called out to the woman behind the counter. "'Allo, Marie. Three specials."

"What is the special?" Ashley asked hesitantly.

"Always good, I guar-ron-tee." Aunt E winked back at her.

The simple food at the café tasted better than a gourmet meal to KC. Finishing the last of her food, she left a tip on the table, then paid at the counter. Aunt E and Ashley had gone on ahead to window shop. As she was catching up, she noticed that the men on the bench were gone and so were most of the cars that had been parked along the streets. She hurried to where Aunt E and Ashley were admiring a piece in an antique shop.

Unlocking the car, KC unleashed her curiosity. "Where is everyone? Is it a holiday, or do they roll up the sidewalks in the afternoon?"

"If business isn't biting, maybe the fish are. Spring fever infects even the strongest man." Aunt E smiled at her from across the car roof.

"Let's hope that Janko and Tyler have been as lucky as we've been," KC said as she started the engine.

Driving back, the women's chatter about the day's events lulled. The sun streamed though the window, combining with lunch, and exhaustion acted like a powerful sleeping pill on KC. She turned the air conditioning on high, hoping that would help keep her leaded eyelids open. Aunt E's hand rested on her shoulder, and Ashley's "Mom!" roused her when she missed the turn to Janko's private road.

Staying awake became her sole focus, so she didn't see the car come up from behind until it was too late. The light gray sedan moved left as if to pass only to strike their car on the left rear panel. The impact sent them spinning down the gravel road. Her heart lodged in her throat as she fought the wheel. Cranking the steering wheel to counteract the slide, she panicked when the car refused to respond. There was no way she could slam on the brakes without risking a rollover that could send them into a tree, or even worse, the black water just a few feet away. Feeling powerless, she hung on until the car jerked to a stop on the narrow strip of marsh grass.

"What the hell?" she roared as she charged toward the offending vehicle. The settling dust clogged her eyes and throat.

The scream that split the air filled her with dread. She'd heard one like it not a month earlier at the county fair, but oh God, this time it came from *her* child.

"Mother, help me!"

KC whirled to see a man dragging Ashley away. "Let her go you asshole." She reached into her waistband for a gun she didn't have while her daughter struggled to stop the man from tying her hands behind her back. When she refused to stop, he hit her.

"You bastard!" Rage blazed through KC, blinding her to good sense as her mother's instinct kicked into overdrive. Charging past their car, she glanced inside to see Aunt E slumped on the seat with blood trickling across her cheek. She didn't have time to check on her now, the man was moving again. This time, toward her.

She could see the fear in her daughter's eyes. "Let her go."

"Now, why would I want to do that? I've got what I want." He stepped sideways enough so she could see his face.

"Arthur." She recoiled as if she'd seen a ghost.

"Hello again, KC. Bet you thought I was dead." He jutted out his chin and nudged Ashley forward a step. "Yes, staging my own death was a stroke of genius. Couldn't have done it without you."

"But I identified your watch."

His maniacal laughter sent chills through her.

"New Orleans has one less greedy man. He was nearly as stupid as you and Jerko. Why you thought you could match wits with me is beyond all logic. Tut-tut, more's the pity. Once you thought I was dead, all I had to do was wait."

Would her nightmare never end? "How?"

"You two are such fools. I followed you to the airport. Airplanes have tail numbers, and numbers can be traced. I knew the right time would come." He snaked an arm across Ashley's middle, his hand dipping past the waistband of her shorts.

She screamed. The earsplitting noise echoed through the bayou, hanging like the moss on the trees. KC took a step, ready to kill the man who'd once been her mentor.

"Uh, uh, uh." The gun in his hand waggled with each syllable. "Look closely at our daughter. See the cell phone?"

She saw the short black flip phone clipped to the waistband of Ashley's shorts.

"Looks like an ordinary phone doesn't it? Well, to some extent, it is. An ordinary phone, I mean. Except this one has an extra battery pack rigged with C-4." He kissed the top of Ashley's head. "Daddy loves you, but you've been a bad girl. You have to learn to listen to Daddy, and when you don't, Daddy will have to punish you."

"Let go of me, you rat bastard. Like hell you're my father." Ashley spat the words at him.

Sandusky jerked the girl's arms up, making Ashley yelp.

KC stiffened, her muscles bunching for an attack. She took a step forward.

"Don't be too quick to rush in." He nodded toward the phone. "The blast may, or may not kill you, but it will blow our pretty little girl in half."

And you'll be dead, too, you son of a bitch. "Please don't hurt her. Why don't you take me and let her go?"

"Oh, I plan to have you both." He motioned toward

his car. "Get going."

An icy, inner calm enveloped her, just like when she worked for Pegasus. Even though she didn't have a gun, she knew she could take him out. He would make a mistake, or she'd force him too, and either way, she'd be ready. Her long shadow stretched between them. "What if I don't?"

He stood in front of her, just out of reach, holding Ashley back so KC could see the other phone attached to his belt. "You are going to do what I want, when I want, and whatever I want, whore, because all I have to do is hit redial to ring the other phone, then push nine. The tone will set off the bomb."

His eyes were cold and soulless as he stared at her. She met his gaze for a moment before turning to Ashley.

"It's okay, Mom." She smiled weakly.

"It's okay, Mom," he parroted.

KC ached to ram her fist down his throat and make him choke on his words. She schooled her features to remain stony while her mind whirled as she filtered action scenarios.

A bush on the edge of the bayou swayed, catching her attention. Did she really see it move? A flicker of hope ignited within her. She needed a miracle. She needed Janko. *Oh, please, let it be him and not an animal or my imagination.*

She kept her eyes centered on Ashley, but watched as the bush wiggled again. Yes, she screamed mentally, wanting to triumphantly pump her fist in the air, but only gave a slight nod with her head. She smiled at her daughter. "I love you."

Both of you.

This was the break she'd been waiting for. Inching closer, she squared her body to Sandusky, controlling her impulse to attack *now*. She'd use every skill she'd learned as an agent, but her best asset was being a woman. A cunning and manipulative woman. Allowing tears to fill her eyes and her lips to quiver, she forced her voice to waver, "Why are you doing this?"

"Because I wanted my rightful family." He stuck the gun in the waistband of his pants before leaning confidently against the car. By hooking his finger in the back belt loop of Ashley's shorts, he positioned her to block the sun from his face, then commanded her to stay.

"I'm not a dog you give orders to," she snarled.

Yanking hard on her shorts, he threw her off balance and into him. "Watch your mouth! You need to be taught some manners. Piss poor job you've done raising our daughter, KC."

She shifted her weight and Sandusky held up a finger.

"Don't do something stupid, although you already have. And you don't even know it."

She watched as the cruel lines around his mouth multiplied his artificially taut skin became blotchy, his predominant forehead, made more so by the receding hairline, flushed, and his glazed eyes sank deeper into his skull. Arthur Sandusky was a madman and she'd never be able to erase the way he looked now from her memory.

He took a deep breath, letting out a long impatient sigh. "Oh, KC, if you'd have only loved me instead of him. I thought that if I were rich and powerful, you would see how much I loved you."

"Arthur, you're married. What about Viola?"

Sandusky continued as if she'd never said anything. "But *he* kept getting in the way. Stealing your affections when you first came on board. I knew he wasn't good enough for you, that you'd become just another of his conquests. He blinded you so you couldn't see how much I adored you. I had to get him out of the way so you could see how I was the best man for you."

Toying with his fingernail for a moment, he flicked whatever was on it away, then examined the remainder of his nails. He kept talking, his voice devoid of emotion. She wanted to puke.

"I'd planned for Osprey to do the job—you know,

killing two for one—but those bozos couldn't get anything right. So they had to go. Cost me plenty, too, although I did get a nice bounty for the feds that were iced. I thought all was lost until *he* blamed you for Osprey's failure.

You came to me that night, that most magical night, and we made love in my room, but you left without a word, without a note telling me of your plans. I thought you were scared and that if I found you, you'd share in my dreams. I longed to create the ideal family for you, as I knew you'd created a new life for me."

He nuzzled Ashley's face, grabbing her to him as she tried to pull away. "You should have known I'd have wanted to experience the magical time of your pregnancy and birth of my only child. You both would have lacked for nothing. I'd have given you all the riches in the world. If only you had loved me as I'd loved you."

KC felt the color drain from her face as she shook her head as his words sunk in. "Oh, God, no." Sandusky had been a mole. He'd been responsible for Osprey's failure. He'd sacrificed her team and Janko's to show her his love. No. No. This was all too horrible. No one could be this twisted. "Arthur, you have it all wrong."

****

Janko lurked behind a wax myrtle bush at the edge of the bayou. His tennis shoes were slowly disappearing in the sucking black muck. Moving quickly and silently had become almost impossible. The danger here was high and he needed his speed. After beaching the boat, he'd had to skirt one alligator nest, and the all-too-close hiss reminded him that others were near.

When KC maneuvered Sandusky's back to him, she'd acknowledged his presence, giving him the opportunity to close without notice.

"Good girl." She *was* trusting him with their lives, and he was trusting her to lead the attack. They were working as a team again.

And damn, that stoked him.

Slipping off his shoes, he crept from his hiding place

to the other side of the car. He caught only bits and pieces of what Sandusky was saying, but could hear KC. The cry in her voice roused him to action, his gut told him to hold firm. It took all the fortitude he had to make himself wait on her signal.

"Don't tell me I'm wrong," Sandusky shouted. "I'm never wrong. Janko thought he'd hidden you so well, but I knew I'd be successful. When the national news broadcast the tractor blowing up at the Cherokee County Fair, Viola thought she saw a woman who looked like you. My short round frigid wife never could stand you. Her loss in the end. I got a copy of the tape from the local affiliate and sure enough, there you were. And that's when I found out you had a daughter. Our daughter. If you'd really loved me, you would have told me. You knew where I was all along."

Janko crouched by the back bumper, able to see all three of them. Like a snake, he was coiled, ready to strike. KC moved nearer. Had she seen him yet?

"I'd always loved you like a brother. After that terrible day, I did go with you, and you were a great comfort, but we never made love." Her voice was stronger, louder.

"Yes, we did. I remember you taking off my clothes, putting your hands on me, loving me. I woke up naked and hard. There was proof on the sheets, and, and—"

"Arthur, you drank so much that it made you sick. I got you out of your dirty clothes, cleaned you up, then put you to bed. That's all. I couldn't have slept with you that night. I'd been shot and couldn't risk discovery. I had to leave to save myself, and Ashley. She's *not* your daughter."

Keep personalizing, KC. You're doing great. Hang in there. Janko willed his encouragement to her.

"That's a lie. You just want to keep her for yourself. She's mine. All you have to do is look at her." Sandusky grabbed the girl's arm spinning her a few steps away from him.

"Yes, Ashley takes after her father in many ways, and I'm very proud of her. But she's not your child."

Janko heard her draw in a ragged breath.

"I was already pregnant. I'd just confirmed my suspicions the night before Osprey went down."

Blood pounded in his ears so loudly that Janko couldn't hear. As if a rug had been pulled out from under him, he fought to keep his balance. Was she saying that Ashley was his daughter? His child?

"Mom?"

Ashley's pleading voice brought him back. Why hadn't KC told him? Why had she kept him away from his child?

"Nooo!" Sandusky howled like a wounded animal. He plucked the phone from his belt, holding it one hand, his finger hovered over the keypad. "If I can't have her, neither can he. Or you."

"Please don't kill her." KC rushed him as she yelled, *"Showtime."*

Janko rocketed over the car trunk, knocking Ashley to the ground as KC lunged for something in Sandusky's hand. He heard the gun go off.

"Get it off me, it's a bomb," Ashley screamed from beneath him.

Flipping her over, he ripped off the cell phone, then hurled it into the grass. "Run, Ashley. Get out of here." He launched her on her way, then scrambled to his feet.

KC's hands were on Sandusky's upraised wrists, and she was using her height advantage to pin him against the car with her body. Suddenly, he head butted her, pushing her back a step. Janko ran up as Aunt E slammed her purse into Sandusky's back.

The jolt broke KC's grip and she fell as Sandusky staggered into Janko's waiting right hook. Art's head snapped back as spit flew through the air. Consumed by a black rage, Janko let loose a flurry of punches, ending with a left into the mid-section that lifted his one time contemporary off the ground. He followed that with a right that sent the bastard reeling into the bushes.

Janko drew in labored breaths. He became aware of the anger ebbing, along with the adrenaline as he stood at the feet of the man he'd once called a colleague. He sensed KC, Ashley and Aunt E behind him, watching for his next move. And for once in his life, he didn't know what that would be.

Sandusky sat up, his jaw hanging askew from a face that resembled raw meat. He managed to rise on his knees and hold up his arm. In his hand was the cell phone bomb.

"We've got to move." KC's hand tugged on Janko's shoulder, but he shrugged it off.

"No one hurts my family." Ashley stepped forward holding the detonator phone. Her hair had shaken loose from a clip, auburn tendrils swinging with the light breeze. Tears had left trails down her dirty cheeks.

Janko looked at her as if for the first time. He thought of his sister, Sarah, at that age—so young, so vulnerable, yet so strong. He didn't understand why he hadn't seen the resemblance earlier. This girl was *his* daughter and he wouldn't let Sandusky destroy her innocence. "Give me the phone, Ashley."

"No, he tried to kill us." The fierceness on her face relayed the depths of her determination.

"I know. He's a mean man, and deserves to be blown to hell. But you don't want to be the one who sends him there." He held out his hand, but Ashley clutched the phone closer.

"How do you know what I want? Or what I can dish out? You don't know me at all." She sidled away.

But I'd like to.

It was just a small noise, easily missed by those not raised on the bayou, but one that meant trouble. Big primeval trouble. Janko pivoted, his gaze fixed just beyond Sandusky. His warning shout was too late as the huge alligator surged out of the water.

The massive jaws opened as if powered by

compressed air, then snapped closed across the man's hips. The sound of bones snapping gave way to terrified screams that were snuffed out as the alligator slid into the water.

In horror, they watched as he surfaced, his arms clawing in a futile attempt to free himself. His bulging eyes shot them a frightened look an instant before he disappeared.

Janko drew Ashley into him to block the gruesome sight. Sobs wracked her slender body and he put both arms around her. She clung to him, her tears soaking into his shirt and into his soul. His heart embraced her. As terrible as the circumstances were at that moment, he could not suppress the joy that grew inside him. He was a father.

The unexpected and violent explosion shattered the peace that had settled on him. As bits of debris and water rained down, Ashley fled into the safety of KC's arms. Immediately, he missed her warmth. Emptiness seeped in.

Sandusky was gone for good.
So was his faith in KC.

Chapter Thirteen

The roar of engines filled the air. KC put Ashley behind her as she looked across the water. A swarm of airboats rounded a bend in the bayou, then headed their way. Her frayed nerves unraveled a bit more when the crafts zoomed onto land. Five rough-looking men, each carrying an assault rifle, burst on shore, fanning out as the brawniest one walked up to Janko. In the big man's wake was Tyler, acting like a *Mini-Me* with his ball cap on backwards and a bone handled fishing knife stuffed in the waistband of oversized camouflaged pants. He swaggered as he came to her.

"Tyler! Are you all right, baby?" She bent to hug him, but he held out his hand.

"Aw, Mom, not in front of the guys. I'm an official swamp rat now."

"Boy, give your mama dat hug." The gruff man said as he pointed to her.

"Okay, Zeke." Tyler's head drooped with embarrassment, but only momentarily before he grabbed her around the middle and squeezed.

Over the top of his head, KC saw the big man shake Janko's hand, then swoop the diminutive Aunt E off her feet. The other men closed around them, nudging and slapping backs. Laughter filled the bayou.

Her heart lurched. Janko hadn't spoken to her, hadn't acknowledged the fight, or Sandusky's death, or even come close to her or Ashley.

When his family circled about, he lifted his head to

look at her. And that look was deadly. He'd rejected her, and her children, just like she'd feared. She'd read it in the stiffness of his body, the glare from his eyes, the waves of hostility from his thoughts. Her feelings of betrayal threatened to swamp her as if she was sinking into the black water.

"Time to go, kids." As they started toward the house, she draped an arm across Tyler's shoulders. "Hey, Slick, how was your fishing trip?"

In a rushing, breathless voice, he outlined the day, scrambling the time line on some events, and after backtracking a little, she got the gist. Janko was a cool dude. The fishing was okay. The airboat ride awesome, but meeting Zeke was the tightest.

"Zeke nabbed me a baby gator, when we heard *you* scream." He peeked at his sister from around the safety of KC's body. "I told them that was just my dumb ol' sister, and that she can yell real loud, and they didn't need to worry. Janko got a really cranky look on his face and then, he let me stay with Zeke."

"Slow down, son."

"Okay. Did ya know he's Janko's cousin? Then he left."

"Who left?" KC asked.

"Janko did, Mom. Sheesh!" His exasperation was short lived as he got back into his tale. "Then all of a sudden, these friends of Zeke's showed up in their airboats and they start talking, then there was that big explosion! Oh, Mom, it's so cool speeding through the swamp. You gotta try it. Maybe Janko will teach you how to be a swamp rat like he did me."

The hole in KC's heart grew larger. Janko had already taught her too much. She couldn't bear any more lessons from him.

Tyler, his face flush with excitement, was tugging her up the porch steps. She beamed at him, pleased that at least he was happy. "Yeah, maybe. But right now, you smell like a swamp rat. The faster you get a shower, the happier we'll be."

As he scampered in the house, she held the door open for her daughter, but stopped her from going inside.

"Ashley, are you okay? Would you like to talk?"

The blue eyes, the same as Janko's, held hers with a clear steady gaze. And in the same way as Janko, KC saw her daughter draw a curtain across her emotions.

"No, Mom. I think you've said enough." Ashley left her alone on the porch.

"Oh, God, what have I done?" she murmured. How was she going to handle today? And Ashley? It had been a lot for an adult, but was it way too much for a teenager? Kids saw things in black and white with few shades of gray.

Resting her head against a column, she breathed in the heady scent of lilac from the nearby bushes as she looked around. Live oaks stretched their branches over the grass so emerald that the oyster shell driveway gleamed. On the outside, it was so beautiful, so peaceful, and everything she wasn't.

She'd done the right thing while Ashley was growing up. Telling her that her father didn't want either of them would have been far crueler than saying nothing at all.

KC rubbed her temples to relieve the building pressure, but it didn't work. She needed to get away. The sooner they left here, the sooner she'd able think clearly. Make a decision. A decision that would affect the rest of their lives. Right now, she didn't have a clue, but she prayed she wouldn't be making another mistake.

****

Janko watched KC and the kids walk toward his house. His blood still boiled that she'd kept his child from him. She'd robbed him. Stolen what was precious from him. Why didn't she tell him then? He could have changed.

But...

A slap on his back made him aware of the circle of people around him. He noted the curious expression on his aunt's face, and the questioning one on his cousin's. Closing his eyes for a few moments, he walled in his emotions and erased any trace of them from his body.

"Hey, Cooter, tell me 'bout what's gone down." Zeke's dark eyes drilled him.

He wasn't prepared to deal with anyone. Not yet. He had to come to grips with KC's revelations and his own feelings. "Aunt E, let Bud take you go home. I'll only keep Zeke a minute or two."

"I know you're trying to get rid of me. You can run, *mon p'tit*, but you cannot hide—not from yourself." She hitched her 5'2" frame as tall as possible, then pushed back her shoulders. "I'll not leave those *chers*, nor their mama. They need me. And so do you." She turned her cheek to him, which he dutifully kissed. "Ezekiel, *adieu*," she called and the big man bent almost double to kiss her other cheek. The group of men remained silent until she and Bud had disappeared around the bend in the road.

"Cuz, what the fuck happened? And what's *Maman* so upset with you 'bout?" Zeke good-naturedly punched Janko's arm just like he had when they'd been boys.

"Long story. I'll tell you about it one day, but not today. Too much, man, too much. I'm trashed." He surveyed the scene around them. It was more than two crumpled cars, bits of debris, torn up grass and gouges in the earth. Lives had been changed forever. Ashley's, KC's, Tyler's, his...He stood there as clueless as Humpty Dumpty after the fall. How he could put all the pieces back together again? How could he make himself right again?

"Cooter?"

Janko mentally shifted gears into agent mode. "Zeke, I know you and your crew just returned from assignment this morning, but I need a sweeper team."

"Not a problem. If the boys here have too much time on their hands, they get restless." Zeke eyed the fellows behind him as they heartily disagreed. "What do you have in mind?"

"First, Aunt E's car needs to be fixed and returned without notice, then this rental car has to reappear in another parish. Make sure the car agency has no doubts about what became of the driver."

"Casper, you up for this one?" Zeke asked. A young blond man, no bigger than a wisp of wind, materialized at Zeke's elbow.

"You bet, Z." He'd barely spoken the words before he vanished.

Janko permitted himself a brief smile before continuing. "Next, I need a couple of the guys to bag and tag what's left of Sandusky, then send a sample for a DNA report. Send everything to Cheryl Paxton. She'll know how to handle the rest."

"Arthur Sandusky, Director of Personnel?" Zeke whistled his astonishment. "No shit!"

"Yeah, I'm gonna make sure the bastard is dead this time. Someone should stay to make sure any pieces that float up are never discovered." He tried to keep the hate from his voice, but didn't succeed.

"We're on it," said the taller of the two remaining men, then they headed to their airboats.

When the engine noises had faded from the bayou, Zeke caught Janko's arm. "Cuz, I'm giving you a few days, then I'm coming back with a jug of hooch. Like Granny always said, 'You air your sins to free your soul, boy.'"

"You're on," Janko said as he waved goodbye to Zeke.

Climbing into his boat, Janko slipped into the privacy of his own thoughts as he navigated the channels back to Seven Oaks.

Love hurt. He'd allowed himself to love not only KC, but her children. He winced as if he'd been sliced open. The way he learned about Ashley had rubbed salt in his wounds. For that, he blamed KC. She should have told him about his child, and she should have *known* he'd love Ashley, regardless of what he'd told her.

Now that he knew about his daughter, he wanted to be a part of her life. What if she rejected him? The possibility that she might not want to see him loomed large in his mind. Was it too late?

A raw ache spread through his body. His love for them had made him an easy target. He didn't think he'd survive any more hurt.

Darkness enveloped the swamp, but he didn't need light to know where he was. So why couldn't he have steered his life like this boat? He thought he had until just a few hours ago.

The boat banged against the dock, pitching him forward. He scrambled to regain his balance, then killed the motor like he tried to kill his thoughts. Tying off the bowline, he returned to the house, determined to not let KC leave until he'd charted a new course.

****

Early the next morning, KC grabbed a mug of coffee on her way outside. She wandered into a garden where rose trees stood like silent guards around the arboretum. Blooming flowers and rose bushes in irregular shaped beds, drew her farther along a winding path. The profusion of color tantalized her eye, as if a rainbow had melted over the ground. She passed through islands of fragrance, stopping to smell and touch the velvety petals. Janko used to surprise her with a rose.

She closed her eyes, listening to the hum of bees as the sun warmed her face, not allowing herself to think about what was dead and gone. That would spoil the tranquility of the garden.

"I hate to disturb you—."

"Too late." She opened her eyes to find him staring at her. Her heart skipped a beat. Dammit, he could still take her breath away.

"Murphy's here."

"Murphy? What's he doing here?" A bad feeling settled in the pit of her stomach.

"You'll find out. He shot her a contemptuous look before walking back to the house.

Alone.

She stood as if rooted to the spot, watching his retreating back. The pain of his rejection cut deep into her soul, but she'd wanted to tell him, to explain.

When he'd refused to talk to her yesterday, she chalked up to shock learning he was a father, but today's hostility was—was... *Oh hell! Get over it. It's your own fault, Janko. You told me every chance you got how much you hated kids.*

She fought the urge to cry. No matter how much it hurt, she could never let it show. As she entered the house, she masked her emotions.

The kitchen was empty, but she could hear Murphy, or rather his laugh, from there. Hurrying, she found him standing next to Janko at the far end of the living room. Their attention was focused on something outside.

"Seems like you always have your back to me, Murph." Her voice sounded more chipper than she felt as she made her way around the furniture.

When he turned, she read genuine pleasure in his face.

"That makes me easier to sneak up on. Good to see you, lass."

He enveloped her in a tight hug, then kissed her cheek. As he let her go, she linked her arm with his, forcing Janko to take a step back, or be bowled over.

"It's great to see you again. You'll get to meet my kids." She squeezed Murphy's arm as she drew him over to the sofa, but he didn't sit. Casting him a questioning look, she saw he'd become somber.

Janko had slipped behind them, she noticed, and now stood at the fireplace with his elbow propped against the mantel. His face betrayed no emotion.

No, he betrayed only people.

She eased out of Murphy's grasp, her glance darting between the two as she edged her way across the room until stopped by a coffee table. "Ouch!" She rubbed the side of her knee. Murphy and Janko continued to stare at her as if she was a multi-headed medusa. They moved to form a loose triangle, and she immediately thought of an old western show down. Warning bells clanked inside her mind. "What's going on?"

Quiet—too quiet—the house is too quiet.

"Where are my children?" Panic rose like the bile in her throat. Her breath shortened, her heart beat faster, and her head pounded. Aunt E had assured her last night everything was all right, that they were safe. What was going on?

She followed the direction of their gaze. From the shadows, stepped Sarge.

"I've taken care of your kids." His gravelly voice sent a wave of terror through her.

"If you've hurt them—" She started over the coffee table, ready to leap for his throat, when Murphy hauled her back.

"Whoa, Kelly lass. Settle down."

Even off balance, she struggled to get free. "Lemme go. What have you done to my kids? Is that why you're here? To eliminate us?"

Turning to Janko, she saw the flinty look return to his eyes. "You saved them once, please don't let them die. Ashley's your daughter, too. And Tyler, he—he worships you. Or is this your doing?"

Janko straightened, then nodded to Sarge. "Close the pocket doors and lock them."

After shutting them, he remained there, his arms folded. He stared straight ahead like a mannequin.

Letting out a desperate cry, she fought harder against the steely arms holding her prisoner. Her gaze locked on Janko, the man she'd loved all her life, as he watched her struggle in vain.

"Give it a rest, darlin'," he said impatiently as he came toward her. "Sarge gave the kids a stack of the latest DVDs and headphones, and told them not to disturb us." The air crackled with tension.

Murphy eased her onto the sofa far away from Janko, then sat beside her. His beefy hand patted the red marks on her arm. "We didn't mean to frighten you. No, not at all. I'd assumed that Janko told you last night that we were coming to debrief, to wrap up this mess." Murphy's bushy white brows furrowed. "Are you two at each other *again?*"

Now it was Janko's turn to be under the big man's glare. Murph cleared his throat. "Are you positive that Sandusky is dead this time?"

She shrugged. Her anger had sealed her mouth shut.

Janko gave her a frosty glance before he spoke. "It was a bloody mess down there. Zeke's boys cleaned the area, staying all night to make sure. Zee personally took tissue samples to the lab for DNA verification."

"Zeke's back?" asked Sarge. That was the most emotion KC had ever heard in the man's voice.

Janko looked over his shoulder. "Yeah, got in yesterday morning. What timing, huh?"

Murphy tried to stand up, but his bulk and the soft sofa cushions worked against him. He tried once more then stayed seated. "You can finish your report from here. Send it to me at the agency, or bring it when you clean out your desk, Janko. KC, I want your version, too."

She did a double take, not quite comprehending what she'd just heard. "Murph? You're back at Pegasus?"

"I never left. Well, not really. Went covert for a few years."

"Like twelve or so," Sarge added dryly.

Murph shot him quick glance. "If I hadn't taken leave to be with Betty, then that favor for the Army, we'd never have been such good friends. Harrumph, yourself."

"Murphy is Control, KC." Janko's voice sounded less brittle now. "He formed Pegasus."

Her world turned upside down as her heart ripped open. "Why did you let me take the blame for Osprey?"

Murphy took her cold hand and sandwiched it between his large ones, but it couldn't warm where she hurt so desperately.

"It was my mistake not to tell you. I knew you were

innocent. We were searching for the leak in the agency. Janko convinced me it was for the best. For your safety that I—we—sent you away. I swear I didn't know about the baby until you told me last week."

"Don't you think you should have let *me* decide what was best for me?"

"Perhaps, in hind sight, yes. But you were part of the problem. For years, I'd watched the rivalry between Sandusky and Janko build, then escalate even further when you came. After you left, I thought things had calmed down. I stepped back to run the agency from the outside with Janko as my second in command, and Sandusky as Director of Personnel." A weary sigh escaped him. "That was a big mistake."

She knew there was more, and waited a few moments for him to continue. Murphy looked at her, his eyes filled with tears, his mouth trembling slightly.

"Go on," she finally prodded.

"Sandusky concealed his hatred for Janko very well. As a mole, he became wealthy, but soon the money didn't matter. He wanted to bring Janko down. That meant controlling Pegasus. And having you, if he could. He sold out, or killed, so many agents. Planned all the intricate details himself, and each one different so there was no discernable pattern. From what I've pieced together, he liked to watch the kill, then would erase the killer by some other method. He got quite creative."

Stunned, she didn't want to believe that Sandusky had killed so many of her friends, and had almost destroyed her life. But the truth slapped her in the face.

"Some were mere pawns in a cruel game, others had been hunted like prey. All those lives wasted for the pleasure of one man. I'd suspected Sandusky, but it was only after we found his poor wife had been murdered that I knew for sure."

Janko put his foot on the coffee table, then leaned in, resting his arm on his knee. "Why didn't you tell me?"

"I didn't know who, or how many, he had working for

him. You needed this last mission before you retired. I had to do what was best for my agency. And I'd hoped that by bringing you together, things would finally work out. I'm sorry that it didn't, because I love you like my own children."

The room grew silent. Knowing about Sandusky didn't make what she'd lived through any easier. And "I'm sorry" couldn't make up for all the years of shame and feelings of betrayal.

But the worst part was knowing she'd been cheated out of love, especially by that one special person. No amount of justification could make up for what she'd lost.

Her anger overflowed and she wanted to hit something, or someone. She wanted to scream at the top of her lungs. She wanted out of this room.

Out of this house. Jumping up, she made it to the door before Janko or Murphy could react. "Move!" She pushed Sarge aside, then shoved the doors open. From down the hallway, she heard them hit the stops with a crash.

She found her kids in the back room, and ignoring Tyler's whine to wait until the movie finished, snapped off the TV. Ashley simply stared at her.

"We're leaving. Now."

"Let me go upstairs to get my new clothes." Ashley stepped toward the door, but KC stopped her.

"No. We're not taking anything." She glared at Tyler as he stuffed DVDs in his pants, then waited for him to unload them. As he neared, a DVD slid from the bottom of his pants' leg.

"Mo-om." both kids cried.

She didn't know how they were going to leave, but she'd steal a car, a boat, a horse—anything to get them out. With no firm plan in place and her head pounding as if a jackhammer was inside, she opened the front door.

"What the hell do you think you're doing?" Janko's voice vibrated through her right along side that damn hammer.

"I'm leaving."

"No, you're not. Not until we make some type of arrangement." He blocked her way.

"Arrangement? For what?"

"Not what, who. Ashley. You're not taking my daughter back to Oklahoma."

"The hell I'm not. You hide and watch. She doesn't even know you."

"Then maybe it's about time. You've already robbed me of her first fourteen years, and I'll never forgive you for that."

Years of pent-up anger and resentment came spewing out. "And I'll never forgive you for betraying me."

Toe to toe, nose to nose, neither KC nor Janko gave an inch.

"Don't I have a say in the matter?" Ashley, with tears in her eyes, stood at the foot of the stairs.

KC and Janko's unison "No." made her take a step back.

"Then—" Her bottom lip quivered as she squared her shoulders, "—maybe neither of you should be parents. I'm not a possession to be divided." She ran upstairs and a door slammed, the echo boring into KC's heart.

"Mom?" Tyler's voice came out weak and shaky.

"It's okay, son. Go back and finish your movie. I'll come when it's time to go." The look he gave before he left tore at her already beaten up heart. She was breaking her promise to herself and hurting her children. "I'd better go talk to her."

"No—" he held up his hand, "—let me." Inhaling deeply, he slowly let it out. "Please, give me a little time alone with her. I promise I'll make sure you get to wherever you want to go."

She nodded. He gripped the stair rail and each step was slower and heavier than the preceding one, as if it were painful to walk.

Deep in her heart, she knew he would have been a good father.

****

Janko leaned against the fender of his car, an idle cigarette burning between his fingers. A pile of butts had grown beside the front wheel as he continued to stare at the sky.

His plane had taken off for Oklahoma hours ago. Never in a million years would he have thought he could love KC this way again. And he'd have bet a million dollars that he'd never allow her into his heart this way again.

But he was wrong—big time wrong.

With dusk came the onslaught of mosquitoes, forcing him to leave. The drive back to Seven Oaks was one he could have driven in his sleep, but not tonight. Four times, he discovered that he'd missed a turn. He stopped his car, getting out at the spot where Sandusky had died. The spot where he learned he was a father. The spot where he'd almost lost his daughter.

He kicked a tuft of marsh grass, not surprised to watch a snake run for the safety of the bayou. That's where snakes in these parts belonged, just like Sandusky.

Returning to his car, he opened the door, but didn't get in. Instead, he slammed his fist on the top. "Damn! Damn, damn, damn." He'd made mistakes before in his life, but not like the ones he made today. The first one was taking his anger out on KC. The biggest one was letting her go without saying he loved her.

Hostile and uninviting—that's how Janko viewed his house from the driveway. Inside was no better. The moonlight coming in the windows cast fingery shadows that waited to point out his failings. He went into the parlor, grabbed the bottle of vodka and a glass from the bar, then left.

The wind picked up. A branch scraped across a window and an eerie lament wailed through the structure as if something, or someone, was dying. His footsteps on the creaking floor echoed down the hall as desolation echoed in his heart.

His wandering stopped in the back room where his kids had been in last. He thought of Tyler as his, just like Ashley. And why not, he reasoned while sinking into the deep leather couch. He loved him, too. Did that make him crazy like Sandusky?

Probably.

He poured the vodka, then took a drink. The alcohol burned a hot trail down his throat, and his eyes began to water. At least, that's what he told himself as the tears slid down his cheeks.

The relentless *tick tick* of the grandfather clock in the foyer grew louder. He'd watched KC playing with her kids. The hugs, the gentle teasing, not quite so gentle from Ashley to Tyler, the love the three of them so generously shared, brought home the hollowness in his own life. He missed having a family, and he missed what could have been.

The bottle, now empty, lay on the couch beside the crushed pack of cigarettes. His eyes burned as he stared at the blank big screen TV, then he blinked hard. His remembrances of earlier today seem to materialize on the set as he watched KC, Ashley and Tyler walk to his plane. Tyler had come back to give him a hug. Warmth centered in his chest, and Janko crossed his arms, trying to recapture those last few moments as the boy had rested heavily against him. But his arms were empty now. Ashley, his beautiful daughter, had stopped at the steps to wave. He'd returned her wave. His hands were now leaden and stiff.

And KC, her head held proud and high, didn't look back at all.

Fool. Idiot. Several more names crossed his mind, ending with KC's favorite, "heartless prick."

He cradled his aching head in his hands as he let out an ironic laugh. As for loving KC, he'd tried to stamp it out, delete it from his memory, but it was impossible. He loved her. Sandusky had failed to kill the woman he loved, but Janko had succeeded in killing her love.

Probably any chance he might have had with Ashley and Tyler, too.

He'd sentenced himself to spend the rest of his life in his own private hell, chained with guilt and remorse for company.

Chapter Fourteen

Janko sat on the end of the dock, a shotgun resting on his lap as his toes cut lazy circles in the water. The recent rains had brought up the bayou, and the snakes, not that he truly cared. There wasn't much that he did care about anymore. Each day was a repetition of the one before that, with days piling upon days. He'd wake up, put one foot in front of the other, then try to find something to keep the loneliness from swallowing him whole.

The bullfrogs croaked in syncopation with the mid-morning songs of the mockingbirds and blue jays. He slapped at a mosquito on his bare chest, his handprint white on his sunburned skin.

Retirement sucked.

He raised the shotgun, aimed and fired at a ripple in the water. The spray cooled him, but evaporated almost instantly. The animal chorus took a short break when the birds flew from one tree to another, and the frogs disappeared, but as the water stilled, the bayou returned to its noisy self.

The last few years at the agency, he'd longed for the time to do nothing, to have no commitments, the freedom of no plans. Now he despised all the emptiness. There was only so much fishing a man could do, and without Tyler it was boring, even if the boy did scare the fish away. Through his young eyes, he'd made the most mundane things become exciting. During those times, Janko glimpsed back at the carefree boy who'd spent every possible moment with *Grandpere.*

As much as he hated to admit it, KC's kids had awakened a part of him that had lain dormant for too long. Their vitality had brought freshness into his stale life, but what he missed most was KC. He couldn't walk through the rose garden without thinking she'd be beyond the next turn on the path. When the realization that she wouldn't be there struck, the flowers would lose their vibrancy and sweetness.

"*Alons, m'ptit,* de snake bite will not cure the heart, or make you smarter."

He turned, gave Aunt E a smile he didn't feel, climbed to his feet, then walked toward her, his shoulders rounded as if all the burdens of the world had been placed there.

"To what do I owe a visit from you?" He kissed her cheek, and she reached up to tweak his.

"Rascal. You trying to sandpaper my face with these scraggly whiskers?" Then pinching her nose briefly, she fanned the air between them. "I see why you didn't come to see Zeke off. You smell like a cooter." Her tone became serious as she linked her arm through his as they made their way to the gazebo. "I haven't heard from you."

"I've been busy.

She walked inside and sat in the shade provided by the thick wisteria vines that encircled the structure. A light breeze tickled the leaves and stirred the heady scent from the grape-like blossoms. "Oh, do tell? The house looks like no one lives there."

Only ghosts and memories.

From the corners of his eye, he saw Aunt E pat the seat beside her. He ejected the few remaining shells from the shotgun before placing it against the white lattice. Scooping the shells from the grass, he sat on the bench beside her.

"I used to think you were such a clever boy, but now, I'm not so sure. Haven't you learned anything from your mistakes?"

He toyed with the shells in his hand for a moment, his stomach tightening into knots. "She lied to me, Aunt E."

"Oh, did she now?"

"She should have told me about the baby the night before Osprey."

"Maybe she had her reasons. Did you give her a chance to explain?"

Jumping up, he shoved the shells into the pocket of his cut-offs, then paced about the small enclosure, finally stopping at the entrance. He leaned heavily against the jamb, staring across the wide expanse of lawn to the tree line that bordered the bayou.

"You let her go without telling her how much you love her, didn't you? How can she trust you after the way you've treated her?"

"The way I've treated her?" He spun around to face his aunt. "She didn't trust me!"

"She trusted you to keep her children safe. She trusted you to save us from that evil man. She trusted you with her daughter's life."

"*My* daughter." Tears formed, stinging his eyes. He pivoted quickly to avoid her seeing his pain. "But not enough to be a part of my daughter's life from the beginning."

She placed her cool hand on his shoulder. "*M'ptit*, she did the best that she could then. The rest is up to you."

He heard a car door close, then the sound of it driving off. The echo faded into the trees and the silence of the bayou spun its cocoon around him.

****

KC stood on the small rise where her house once sat. The burned out shell and scarred concrete foundation mirrored the coldness in her heart. Looking across the pasture, she watched as the wind rippled in waves through the tall grass. Soon it would be baled, leaving the pasture like a newly mown lawn, clean and ready to grow again.

She wished it were that simple to mow down her memories, tie them together, store them like hay bales, and let her make a clean start. If she hadn't gone to that fair. If that tractor hadn't exploded in front of a group of school children. If the news cameras hadn't been there.

When she rushed in, she hadn't thought like someone who had a past to hide, only of the children. Now, knowing the outcome, she'd do exactly the same thing. Without reservation.

But she'd paid a high price for her actions. Returning to Treaty Hill had been a mistake, too. Randy had disowned them, wanting nothing to do with Tyler. The good citizens treated her differently, like an interloper. She could no longer go anywhere without the onslaught of questions about what had happened, or about her past, or about her future.

Now Janko wanted to be a part of that future, too. The though scared her to death. She could lose her kids again.

When Janko's letter had arrived asking to establish a relationship with Ashley and Tyler, she'd been filled with apprehension. Could she trust him with her children? Only after the kids had badgered her, did she allow them to spend the day with him in Treaty Hill. But she'd refused to be a part of it or even to see him when he picked them up. The ache inside her had gnawed a hole in her spirit while they'd been gone.

But that hadn't been enough. Now he wanted to take them away for the weekend. What if he pushed her kids away just when they started to love him? It was a painful lesson she didn't want them to learn the hard way.

What scared her more was what if they grew to love him?

Fear had snaked through her, making her irritable. She and Ashley had fought over the upcoming visit. KC knew she couldn't stop them seeing him. Ashley had point blank told her that she and Tyler were going, with or without her permission. If KC tried to stop Janko? He'd already proven he could take her children away from her anytime he wanted.

If she hadn't agreed to this visit, she could lose Ashley and Tyler because they were determined to go. Since she did agree, she could lose them to the man who never wanted her. Either way she figured it, she was going to lose.

Instead of returning to Treaty Hill, she should have taken the kids and run, as fast and as far away as she could get. No matter where they might have gone, she knew it wouldn't do any good, and a whole lot of harm.

Those first few years hiding here had been hard on her, always looking over her shoulder, fear lurking in the corner of her mind. No, she wouldn't put her kids through never having roots. Or friends. Or a real family.

Besides, she knew Janko had the money and the resources to hunt them, then he could disappear with them, never to be found.

A red-tailed hawk circled in the early morning sky, letting out a piercing scream. Off in the distance, its mate answered. She wanted to yell, "Why me?" All she'd ever dreamed about was living a normal life with a good husband, kids and a safe, happy home.

Well, she'd gotten her children, and life on the ranch was all right, but the happiness part had eluded her. Life had dealt her some cruel blows and she'd never felt more alone.

Damn you, Janko! Damn you for turning my world upside down. Damn you for changing my life.

For making me love you again.

Movement under a stand of trees drew her attention and she shaded her eyes with her hand. A black and white Paint colt stumbled up onto unsteady legs, then began to nurse his mother. Deuces Wild and her foal were all that was left of her horse business. She'd sold the rest as a way to keep the ranch, but nobody had been willing to take a chance on the feisty mare with the infamous past. An ironic smile tugged at her mouth.

Nobody wanted her either.

Hoping to find some comfort, she strolled toward the pair. Before her life had gotten so screwed up, her morning walks had been little bits of heaven where she could be alone with only her thoughts, her horses, and a cup of coffee.

The grass muffled her steps and left damp streaks on her jeans. The rush of fragrance from the wildflowers was worth becoming dew soaked.

Deuces greeted her with a soft nicker, and KC buried her head in the mare's neck. She poured out her troubles to the only friend she had left. The mare silently listened and her heart lightened.

Taking a handful of Deuces' mane, she vaulted on the mare's back, then urged her into a walk. The surprised colt snorted his displeasure at having his breakfast interrupted, and reluctantly trotted alongside. She used her legs to guide the mare into the open pasture. Her rubber band taut muscles slowly relaxed as she gave herself to the rhythm of the lope.

Last year, she hadn't been able to ride Deuces at all. Now she could without a bridle and saddle. Both of them had worked long and hard learning to trust, of working through the bad to get to the bond they now shared. Too bad they were such failures with people.

Thoughts of Janko sprang into her mind against her will. Her love for him was like a drug. As hard as she tried to kick her destructive habit of loving him, her heart always came back for more. She had a love-hate relationship toward him. She loved him, and hated herself for it.

The colt bumped against his mother's chest and KC realized she'd ridden farther than intended. Stopping at the creek, she allowed the mare to get a drink and the colt to nurse before heading back.

"Let's go home, girl." The mare raised her head, a clump of grass dangling from her mouth. KC signaled the mare to step out. The colt leaped ahead, bucking and kicking up his heels. She watched him enjoying the sunshine, freedom, and life

The mare danced sideways a couple steps. "You want to go, too, don't you?" Getting good handholds in the mane, she gripped tight with her knees, then leaned forward. No other feeling in the world compared to flying across the pasture.

As the trio neared the barn, KC shifted her weight back, easing the horse to a stop in front of the tack room. Swinging her leg over the mare's neck, she slid to the ground. A nose to her back prodded her to open a stall door that Deuces and the colt ambled into.

"Okay, okay, cool your jets. I haven't forgotten." She went inside the tack room, emerging with a hefty measure of sweet feed. "You're gonna get barn sour on me if I don't stop racing back on you."

"Hello, KC."

Startled, she slung feed everywhere. Recognition knotted her belly. "Dammit, Janko, you scared the piss out of me." He stood in the shadow of the doorway. Her heart hammered, but it wasn't all from fright. Seeing him again after so many weeks was as pleasurable as it was painful.

Deuces nickered and KC disappeared to get more feed, scrambling to rein in her emotions. Empting the scoop into the feeder, she patted the mare's neck, then locked the stall door before she faced him.

"Aren't you getting quite a jump on the weekend?" Her words would have sounded more nonchalant if her voice hadn't squeaked in the middle of her sentence.

"We need to talk."

"About what?" Foreboding lodged like a brick in belly. She swallowed hard.

"KC, I've got to know why you didn't tell me about Ashley before Osprey?"

"Does it really matter after all this time?" She could feel the hurt welling inside her as the backs of her eyes stung.

"Yes. It matters a hell of a lot to me. I want to know." The gruffness in his voice seemed to shake the timbers in the barn.

She bit her lip in an effort to control herself, then took in a cleansing breath and let it out before she spoke. "I tried," pain still colored her voice. "But you were so focused on the raid that the timing wasn't right. Then after Osprey you didn't trust me and no matter how much I loved you, my love wouldn't have been enough to keep us together. Knowing your hatred of kids, I didn't want you to feel obligated—trapped—for the rest of your life resenting me, and the baby. Better off alone than hated."

"I'm sorry," he said with remorse. "A lot of things have changed. I've changed."

"I bet," she said under her breath

"I've got a mission proposal for you."

"That's original. The last time you said that to me, you'd taken my kids." Her heart beat double-time. "Not interested."

"You didn't give me a chance—"

"I don't want to know." She shook her head as she backed away, but he reached her with one long step, pulling her into his arms.

"I propose becoming a team again."

Breaking his grasp, she put some distance between them. She couldn't think with him so close. The sun slipped behind a cloud and she shivered. "I'm not going back to that life anymore."

"I'm talking about a partnership of a more permanent kind."

"What do you mean?" Did she understand him correctly? "Are you asking me to live with you?"

"Sorta."

"No. What happens to us when the going gets too tough on you? Are you going to bail out? 'Now you want us, now you don't.' I can't afford to let you toy with us as if we were a yo-yo. I won't put my children through something like that. They need a stable home."

He chuckled as he looked farther down the barn to where quilt pallets lay on square hay bales. "You got that right. They *do* need a stable home, not a home in a stable."

Her cheeks reddened as his zing registered. "I'm doing the best I can."

"I can help. I can take care of things." He moved closer.

"Don't think you can waltz back into our lives saying you can 'fix' everything." In frustration, she poked him in the chest, backing him up a few steps. "Because you can't. You have no idea the problems you've already caused, or the ones that I'm facing."

"I'd like to." He caught her hand and placed it on his heart. "Marry me, KC."

"Why?" Suspicion sped through her mind like a freight train. Her eyes narrowed. What was his motive here? Easy access to the kids?

"Because I love you."

She choked. He said that so convincingly, she almost believed him. Under her hand, she noted the steady rhythm of his heart. God, she loved him, but could she trust him?

But... hadn't she already trusted with her children?

But with her heart?

He'd hurt her so many times before. She jerked her hand away, then put a few paces between them.

"It's not as easy as you think, Janko, especially when kids are involved."

"When has anything between us ever been easy?" Irritation registered in his voice. "What are you trying do, make me run?"

She shook her head.

"Good, because it's not working. I'm through running. I love you. It's taken me seventeen years to get the courage to tell you those words."

"Then why did you send me away?" She turned her back to him so he wouldn't see the tears pooling in her eyes.

"I've always believed that I was responsible for the deaths of my grandfather, parents and sister. It hurt too much to lose someone I loved. So I convinced myself that I couldn't love anyone. After Osprey, I sent you away to protect myself because I wouldn't have survived if something happened to you. But that didn't stop me from loving you."

"I'm afraid to try again. Afraid we won't work out." She discerned his warm presence behind her.

"I'm not. I believe in you." He encircled her with his arms. "More importantly, I have faith in me. We've got to try, KC. Not for Ashley. Not for Tyler. *For us.* I've never failed to complete a mission, and neither have you."

"I just don't know." She closed her eyes. Her insides churned as if in a blender. Her heart said yes, her mind shouted no.

"I brought you something." He moved away but returned to place something in her hand.

She opened her eyes to see a yellow rose, the edges of the petals tinged blood red. Holding it to her nose, she smelled the sweet scent.

"Do you like it?" The rich timbre of his voice vibrated through her. "I created that variety for you. Took me a long time to get the colors right. I never forgot how special you are."

He put his hands on her shoulders and she leaned against him, the rose clutched to her chest. The tears she tried so hard to control slipped out. "I love my rose...and I love you. I've never stopped loving you."

She didn't allow him to turn her around, so he moved to face her. His hand tipped her chin until she met his gaze.

"I love you. God, it feels good to say that." He kissed the tears from her cheeks.

"Oh, Steven, I've missed you." Her fingers shook as she traced the outline of his jaw then she kissed him long, hard and deep.

The mare whinnied separating them. Janko laughed. KC turned, reluctant to leave his warm embrace. "Sorry, girl." She released the catch on the gate and the mare and colt galloped into the pasture.

"I'm a package deal, you know." She smiled at him.

"Package?" His grin widened seductively as he looked her up and down. "I want it all, darlin'. Kids, cats, dogs, horses—here or anywhere in the world as long as we can build a life together."

She hugged him, and noticed the pair of hawks circling above them as they hunted together. Her heart swelled with joy. The sun had chased the clouds from the sky as well as from her. KC had emerged from the shadows, and with Janko was where she belonged.

A word about the author...

Margaret Reid lives on a small ranch outside Dallas with her husband, numerous critters, and kids, who come home when they can. When she's not writing or ranching, you can find her racing her stock car at the dirt track.